DODO ™

FELIPE NUNES

kaboom!™

DODO, May 2018. Published by KaBOOM!, a division of Boom Entertainment, Inc. Dodo is ™ & © 2018 Felipe Nunes. Originally published in Portugal by Mino Editora as Dodô. ™ & © 2015 Felipe Nunes. All rights reserved. KaBOOM!™ and the KaBOOM! logo are trademarks of Boom Entertainment, Inc., registered in various countries and categories. All characters, events, and institutions depicted herein are fictional. Any similarity between any of the names, characters, persons, events, and/or institutions in this publication to actual names, characters, and persons, whether living or dead, events, and/or institutions is unintended and purely coincidental. KaBOOM! does not read or accept unsolicited submissions of ideas, stories, or artwork.

BOOM! Studios, 5670 Wilshire Boulevard, Suite 400, Los Angeles, CA 90036-5679. Printed in China. First Printing.

ISBN: 978-1-68415-168-4, eISBN: 978-1-61398-983-8

DODO

™

Written and Illustrated by
FELIPE NUNES

Lettered by
MIKE FIORENTINO

Cover by
FELIPE NUNES

English Translation by
ALESSANDRA STERNFELD

Designer
JILLIAN CRAB

Assistant Editor
AMANDA LaFRANCO

Editor
WHITNEY LEOPARD

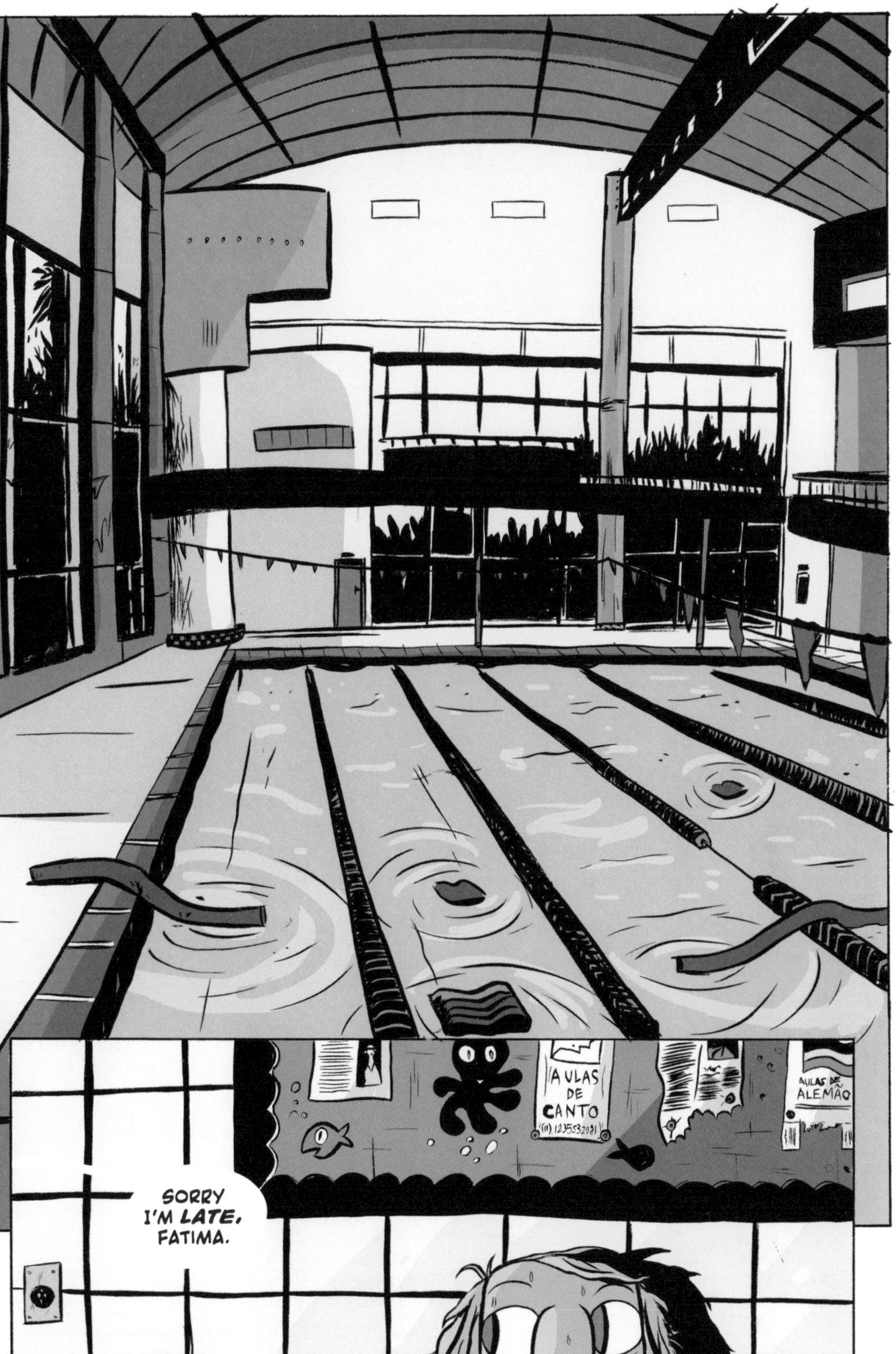
AULAS DE CANTO
(11) 1235532081
AULAS DE ALEMÃO
SORRY I'M LATE, FATIMA.

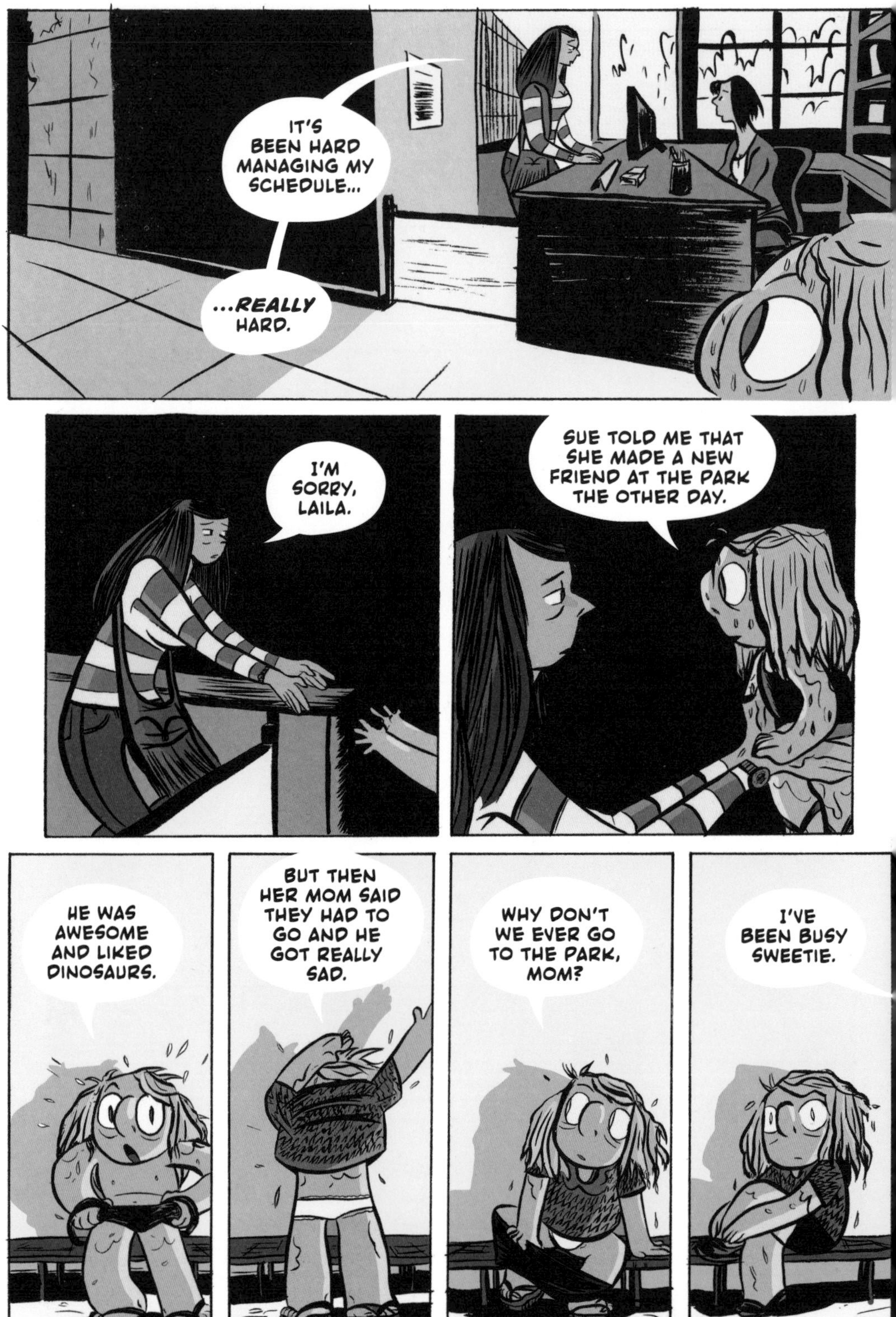
IT'S BEEN HARD MANAGING MY SCHEDULE...
...REALLY HARD.
I'M SORRY, LAILA.
SUE TOLD ME THAT SHE MADE A NEW FRIEND AT THE PARK THE OTHER DAY.
HE WAS AWESOME AND LIKED DINOSAURS.
BUT THEN HER MOM SAID THEY HAD TO GO AND HE GOT REALLY SAD.
WHY DON'T WE EVER GO TO THE PARK, MOM?
I'VE BEEN BUSY SWEETIE.

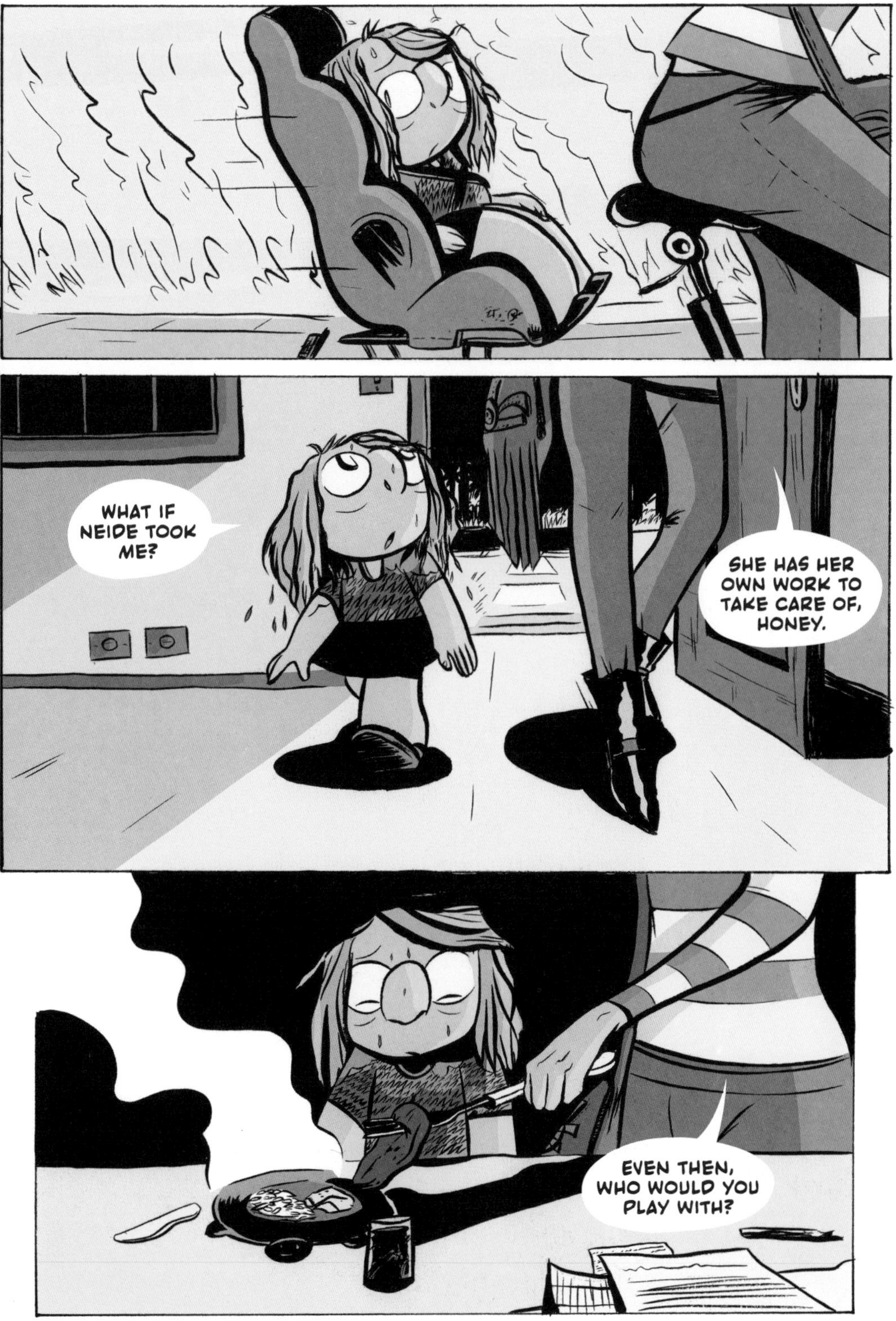
WHAT IF NEIDE TOOK ME?
SHE HAS HER OWN WORK TO TAKE CARE OF, HONEY.
EVEN THEN, WHO WOULD YOU PLAY WITH?

ANYWAY, IT'S MORE FUN HERE AT HOME, RIGHT?

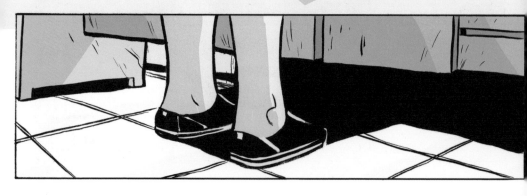

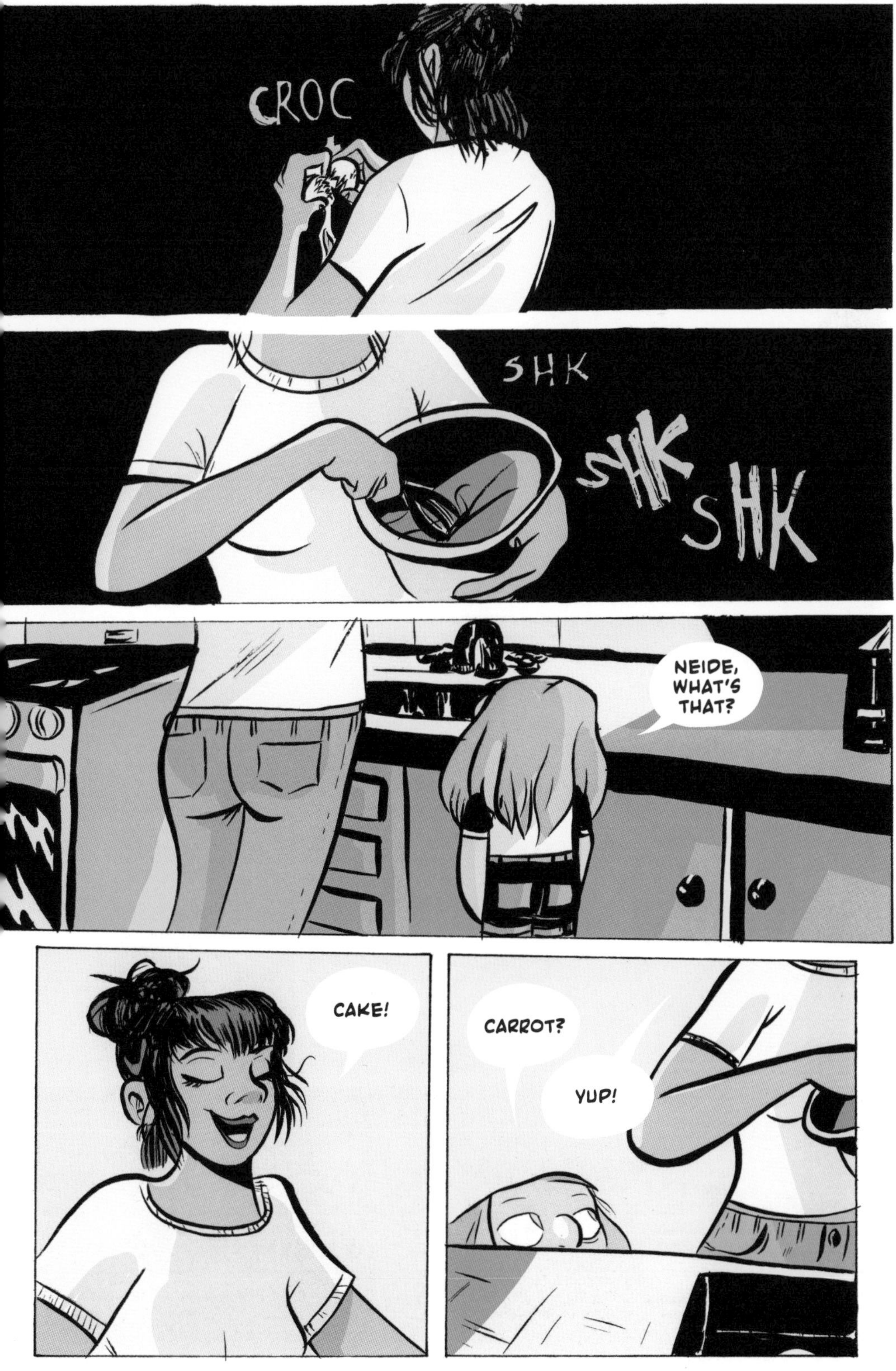
CROC
SHK
SHK
SHK
NEIDE, WHAT'S THAT?
CAKE!
CARROT?
YUP!

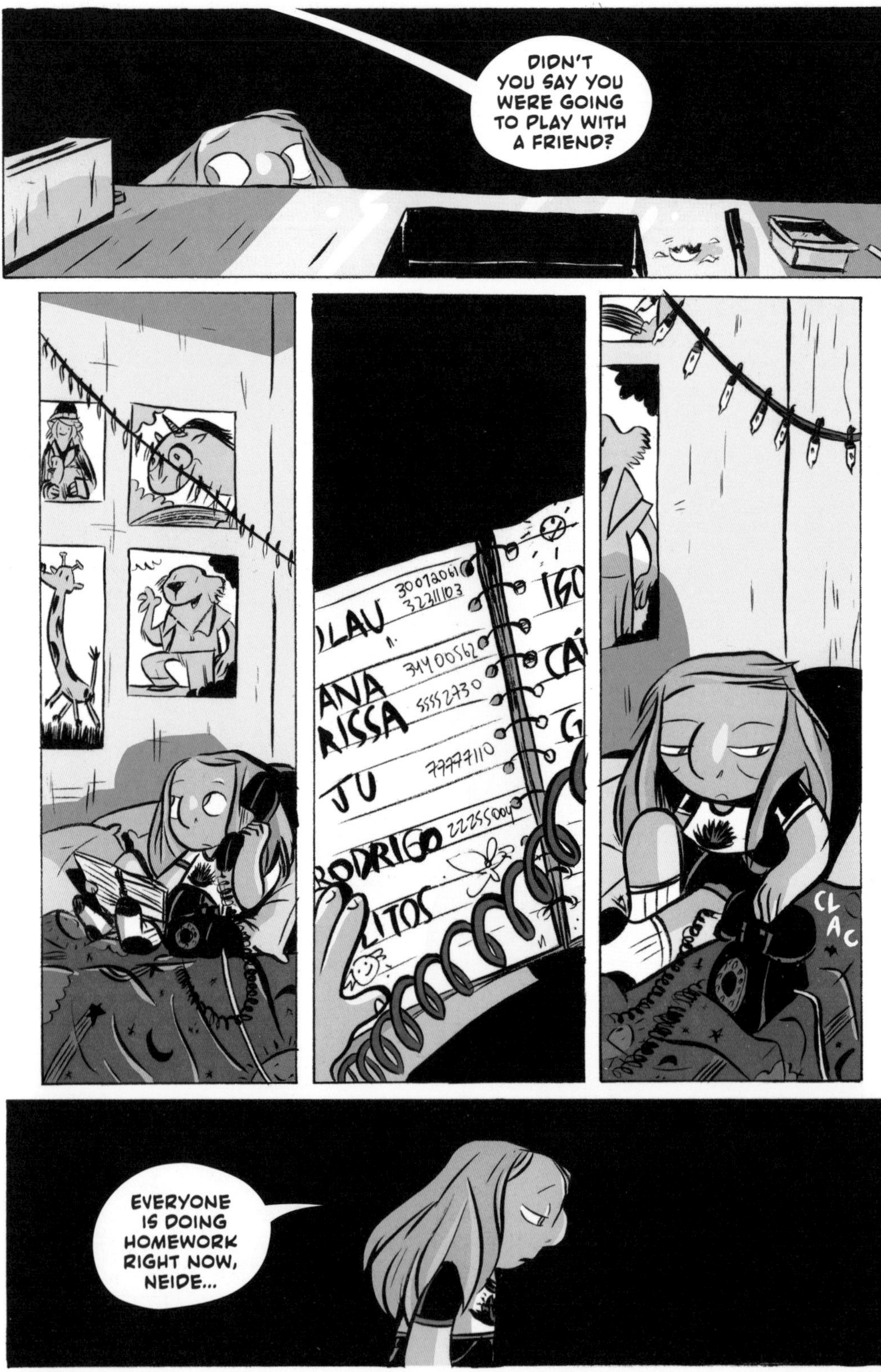
DIDN'T YOU SAY YOU WERE GOING TO PLAY WITH A FRIEND?
CLAC
EVERYONE IS DOING HOMEWORK RIGHT NOW, NEIDE...

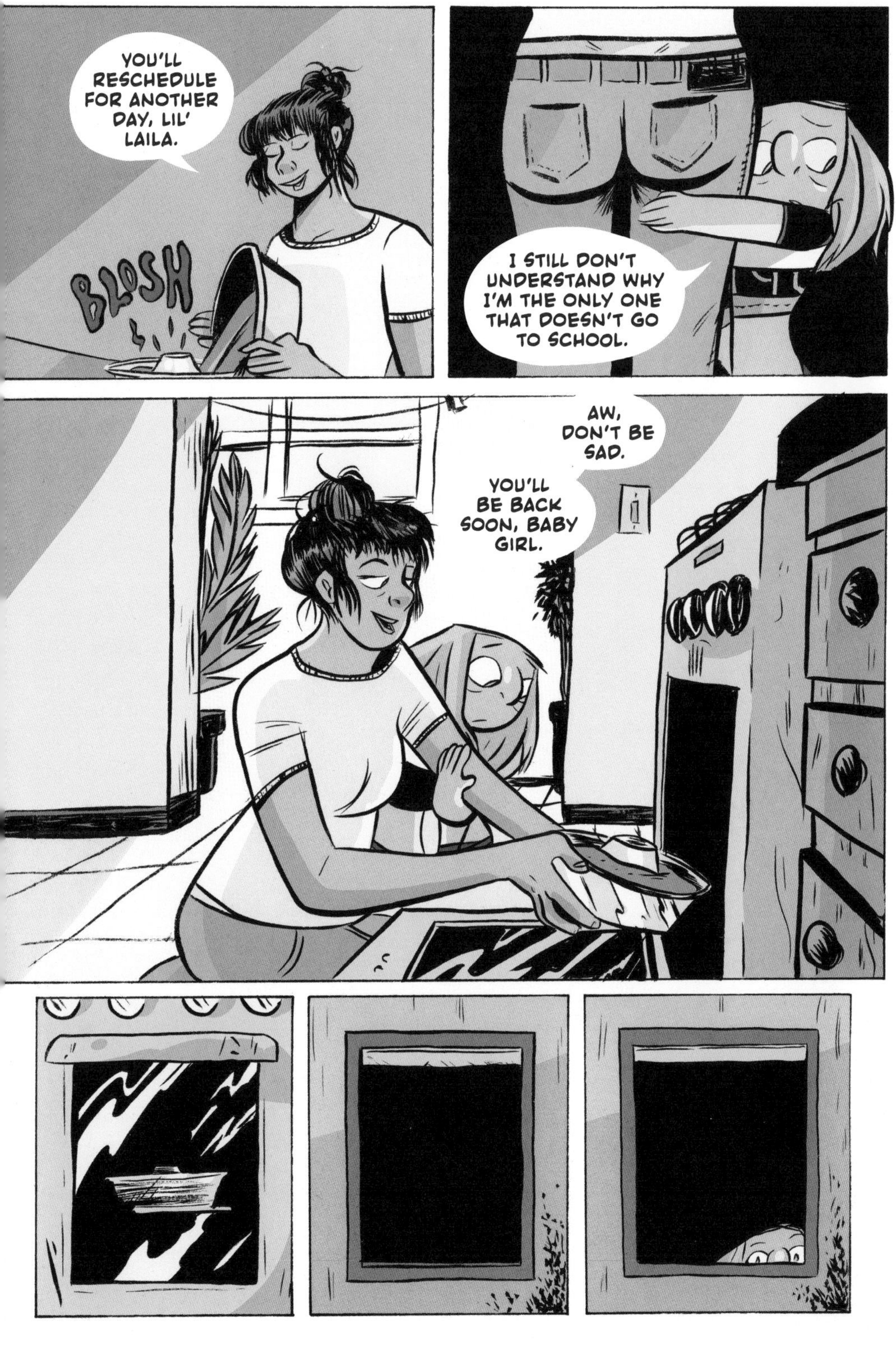
YOU'LL RESCHEDULE FOR ANOTHER DAY, LIL' LAILA.
BLOSH
I STILL DON'T UNDERSTAND WHY I'M THE ONLY ONE THAT DOESN'T GO TO SCHOOL.
AW, DON'T BE SAD.
YOU'LL BE BACK SOON, BABY GIRL.

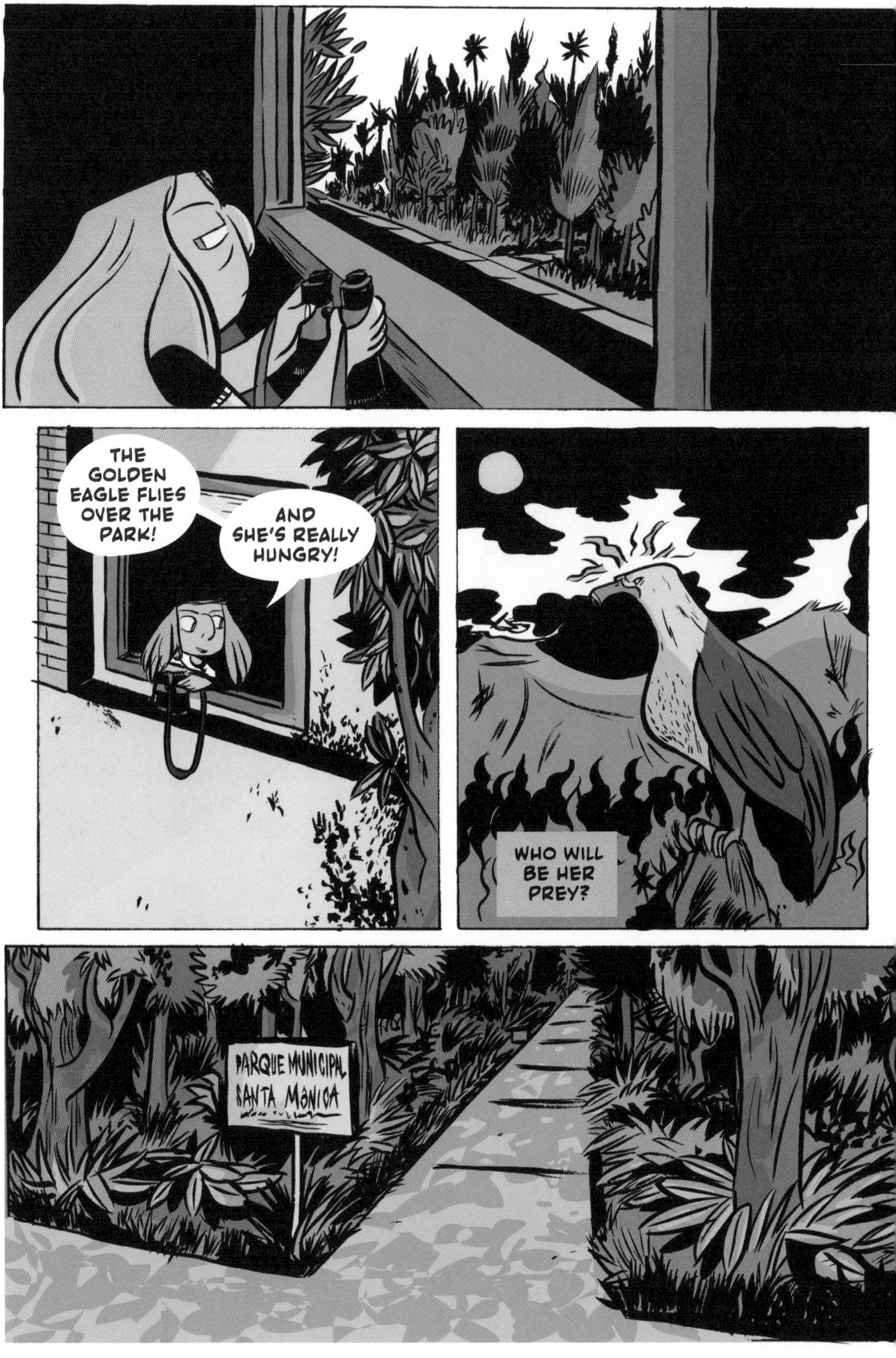
THE GOLDEN EAGLE FLIES OVER THE PARK!
AND SHE'S REALLY HUNGRY!
WHO WILL BE HER PREY?
PARQUE MUNICIPAL SANTA MÓNICA

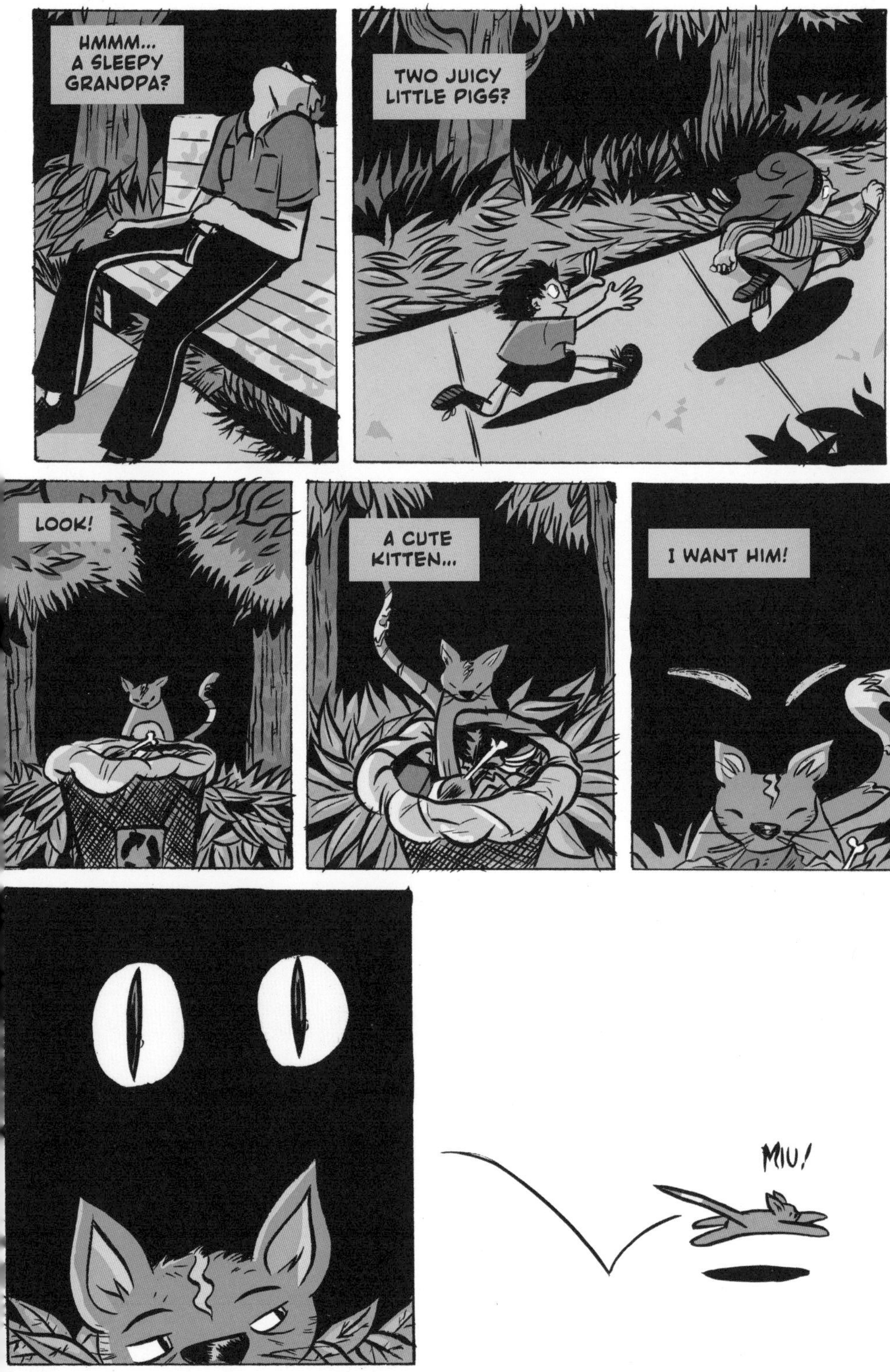
HMMM...
A SLEEPY
GRANDPA?
TWO JUICY
LITTLE PIGS?
LOOK!
A CUTE
KITTEN...
I WANT HIM!
MIU!

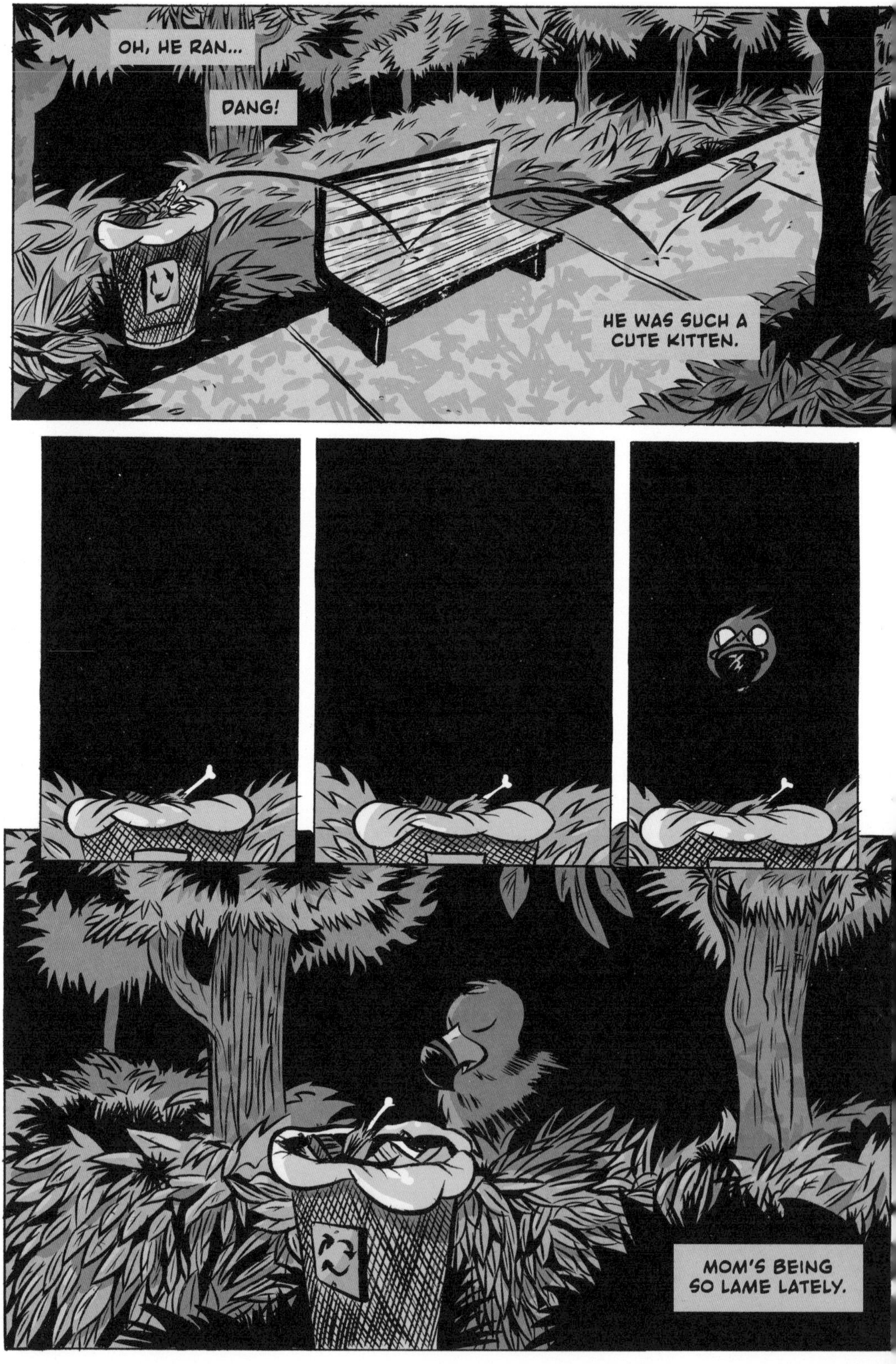
OH, HE RAN...
DANG!
HE WAS SUCH A CUTE KITTEN.
MOM'S BEING SO LAME LATELY.

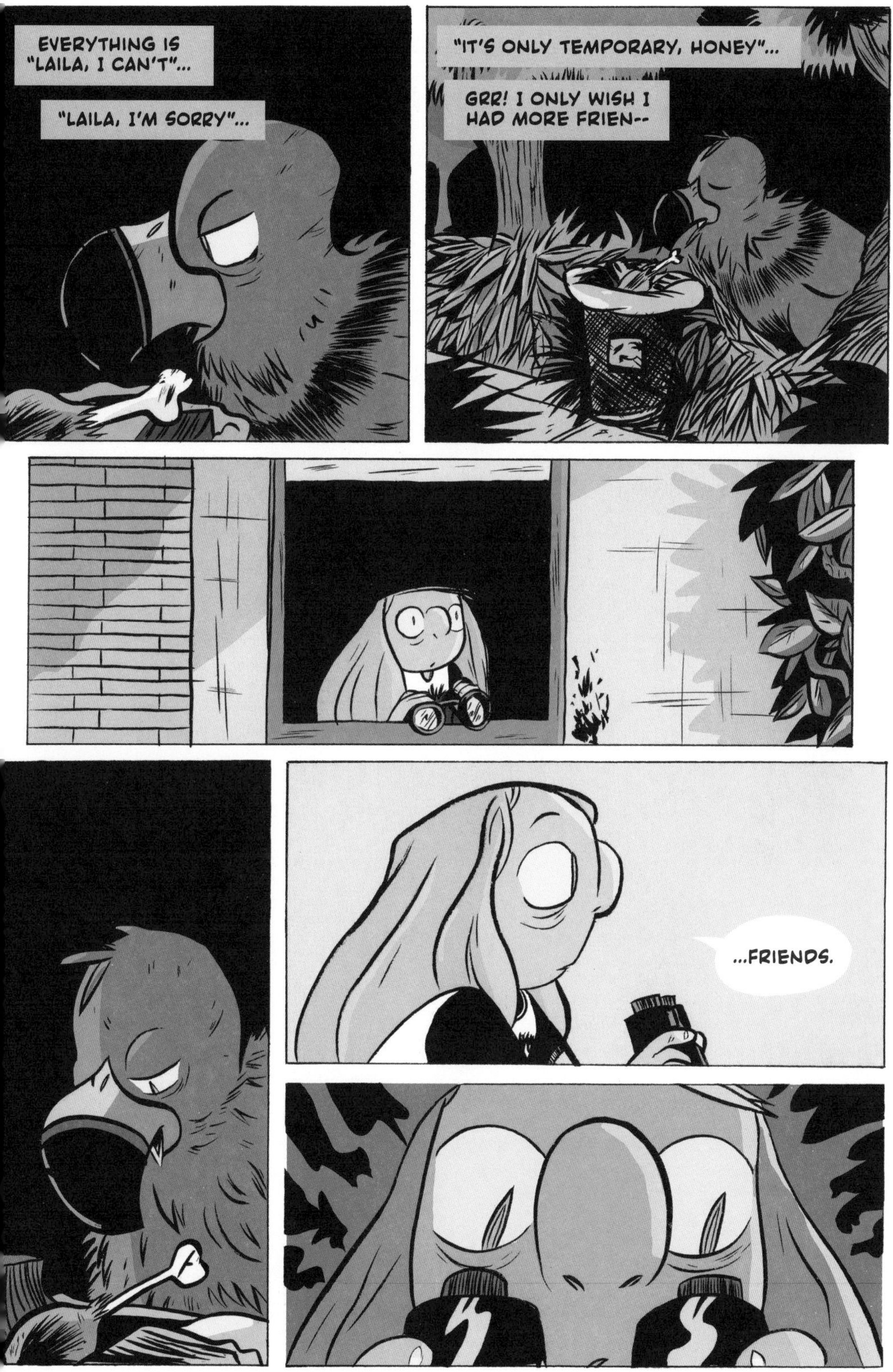
EVERYTHING IS "LAILA, I CAN'T"...
"LAILA, I'M SORRY"...
"IT'S ONLY TEMPORARY, HONEY"...
GRR! I ONLY WISH I HAD MORE FRIEN--
...FRIENDS.

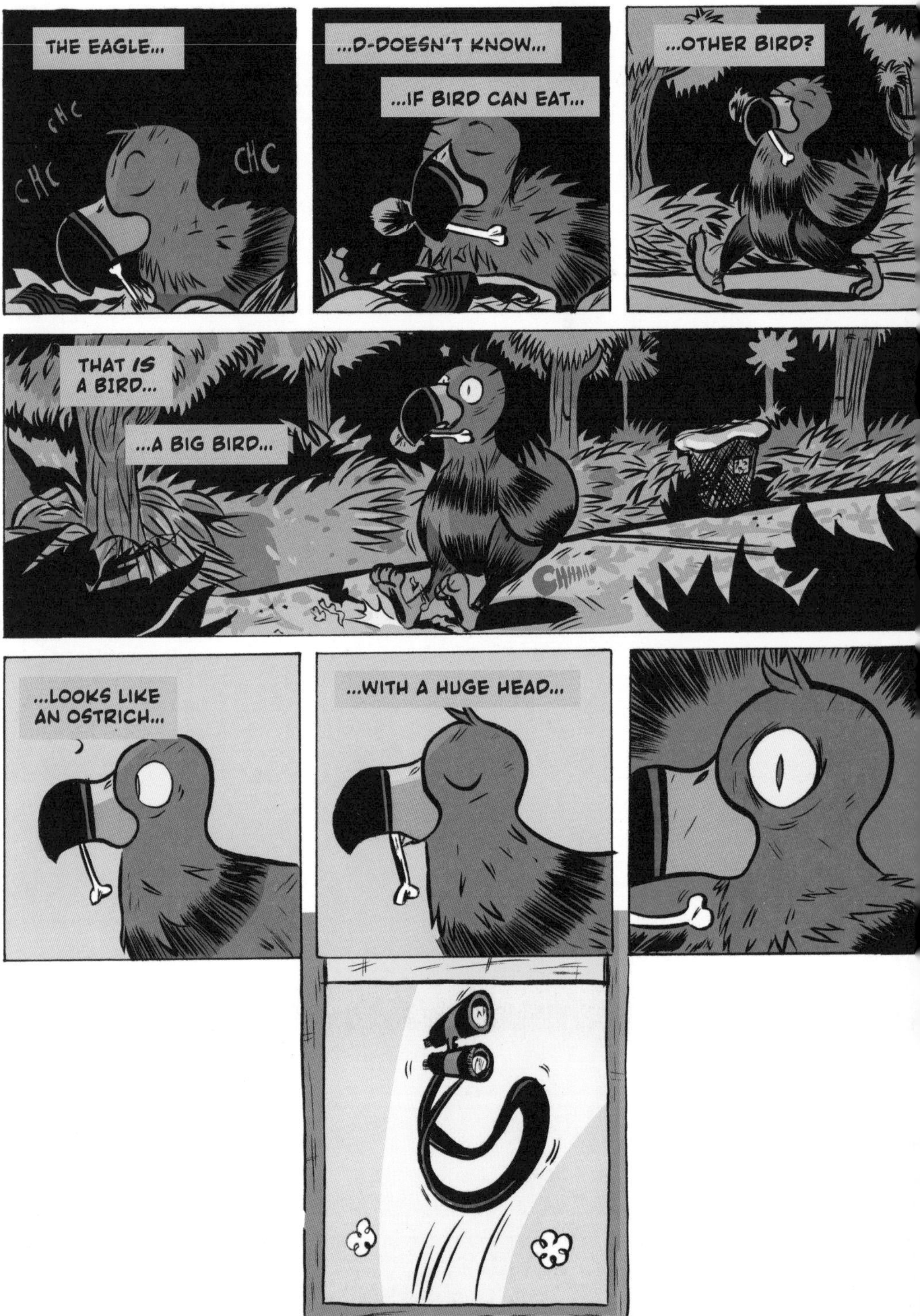
THE EAGLE...
CHC
CHC
CHC
...D-DOESN'T KNOW...
...IF BIRD CAN EAT...
...OTHER BIRD?
THAT IS A BIRD...
...A BIG BIRD...
CHHHHH
...LOOKS LIKE AN OSTRICH...
...WITH A HUGE HEAD...

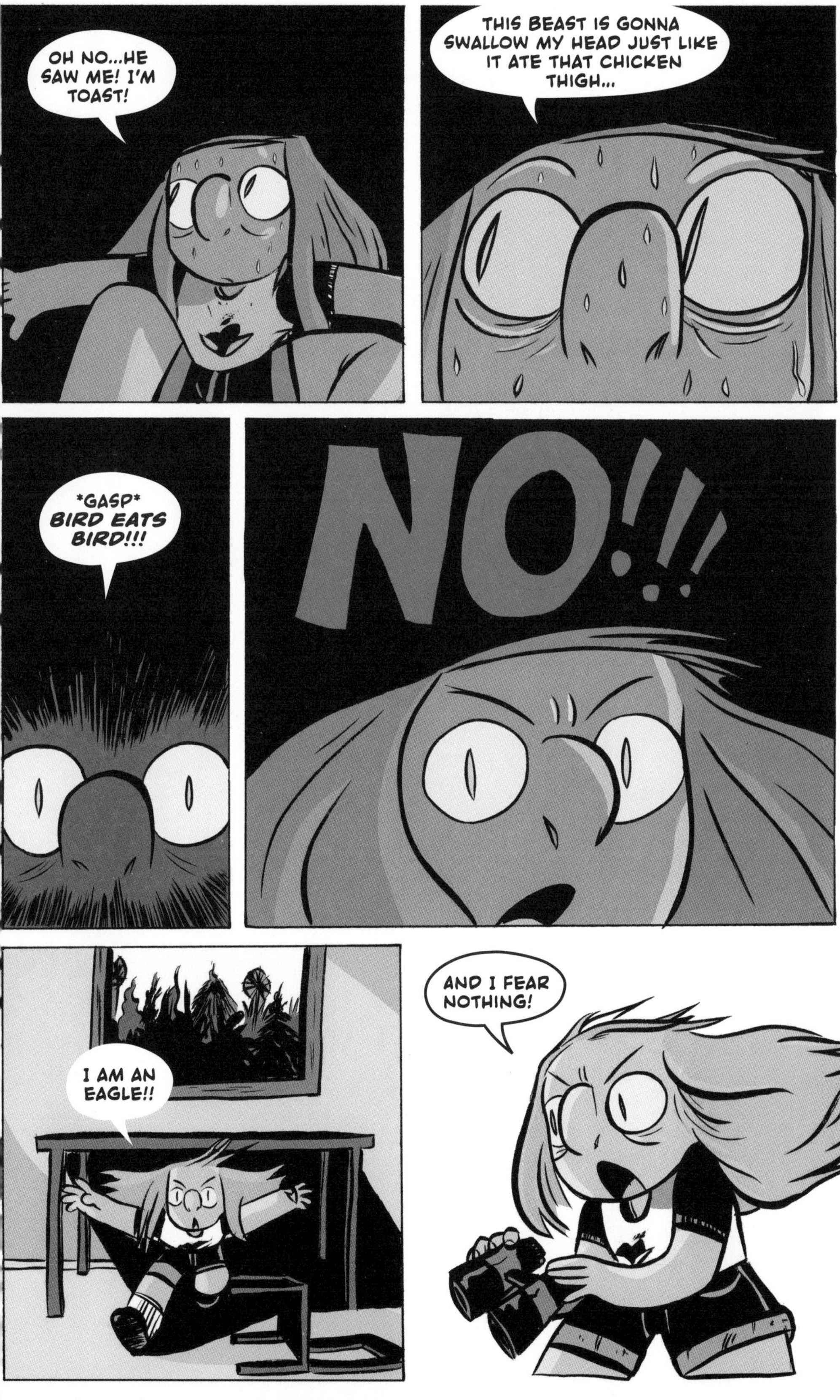
OH NO...HE SAW ME! I'M TOAST!
THIS BEAST IS GONNA SWALLOW MY HEAD JUST LIKE IT ATE THAT CHICKEN THIGH...
GASP BIRD EATS BIRD!!!
NO!!!
I AM AN EAGLE!!
AND I FEAR NOTHING!

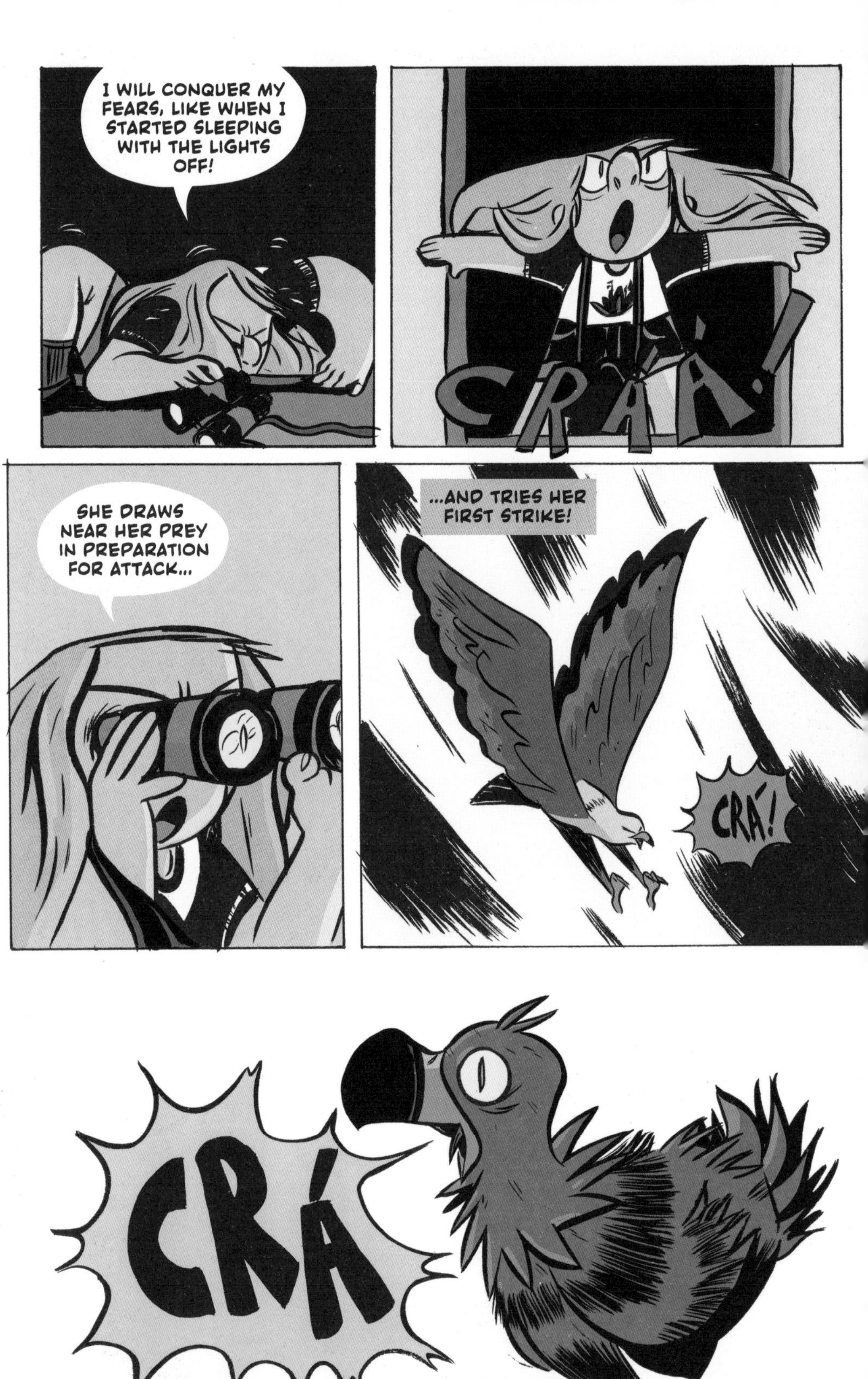
I WILL CONQUER MY FEARS, LIKE WHEN I STARTED SLEEPING WITH THE LIGHTS OFF!
CRÁ!
SHE DRAWS NEAR HER PREY IN PREPARATION FOR ATTACK...
...AND TRIES HER FIRST STRIKE!
CRÁ!
CRÁ

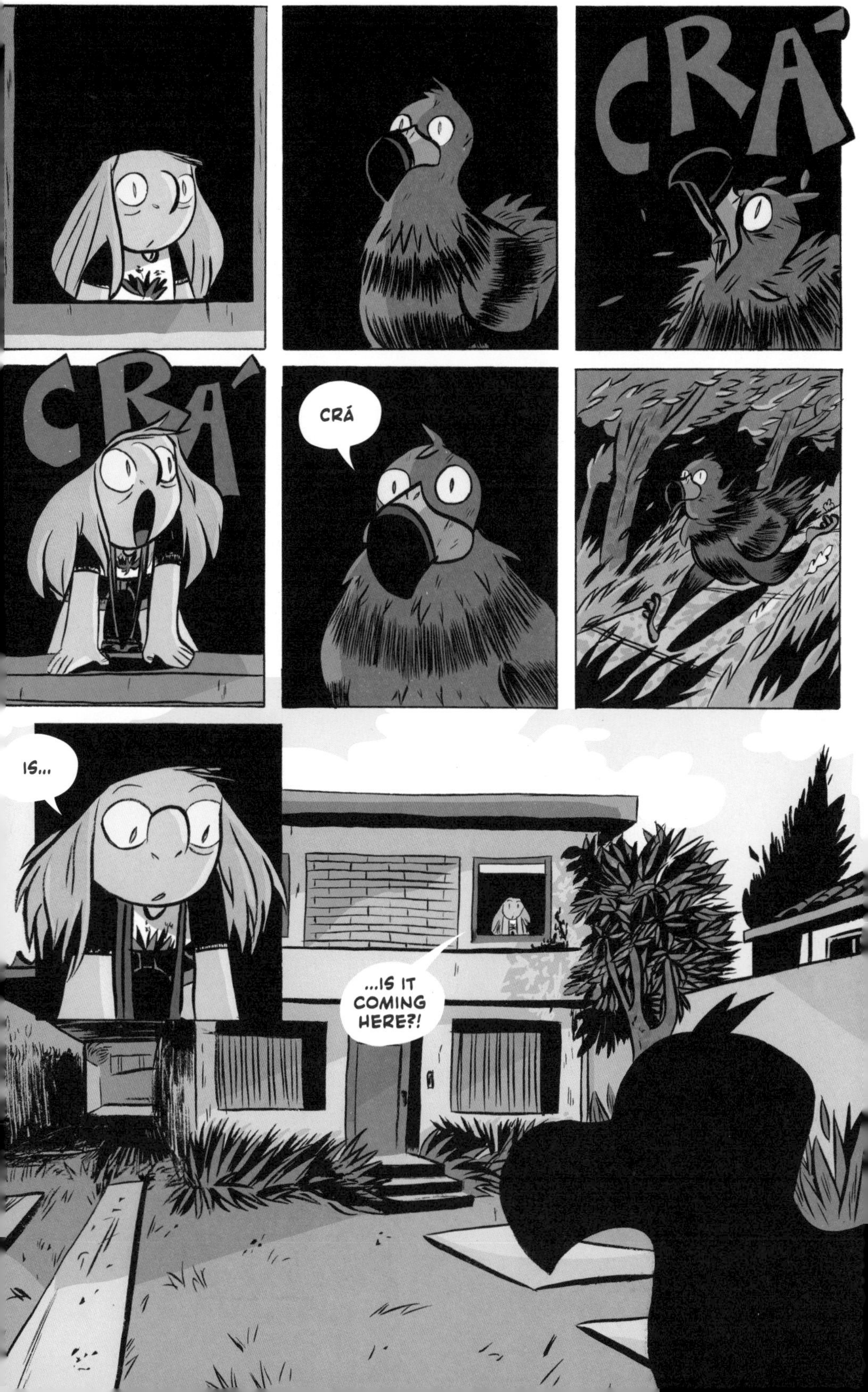
CRÁ
CRÁ
CRÁ
IS...
...IS IT COMING HERE?!

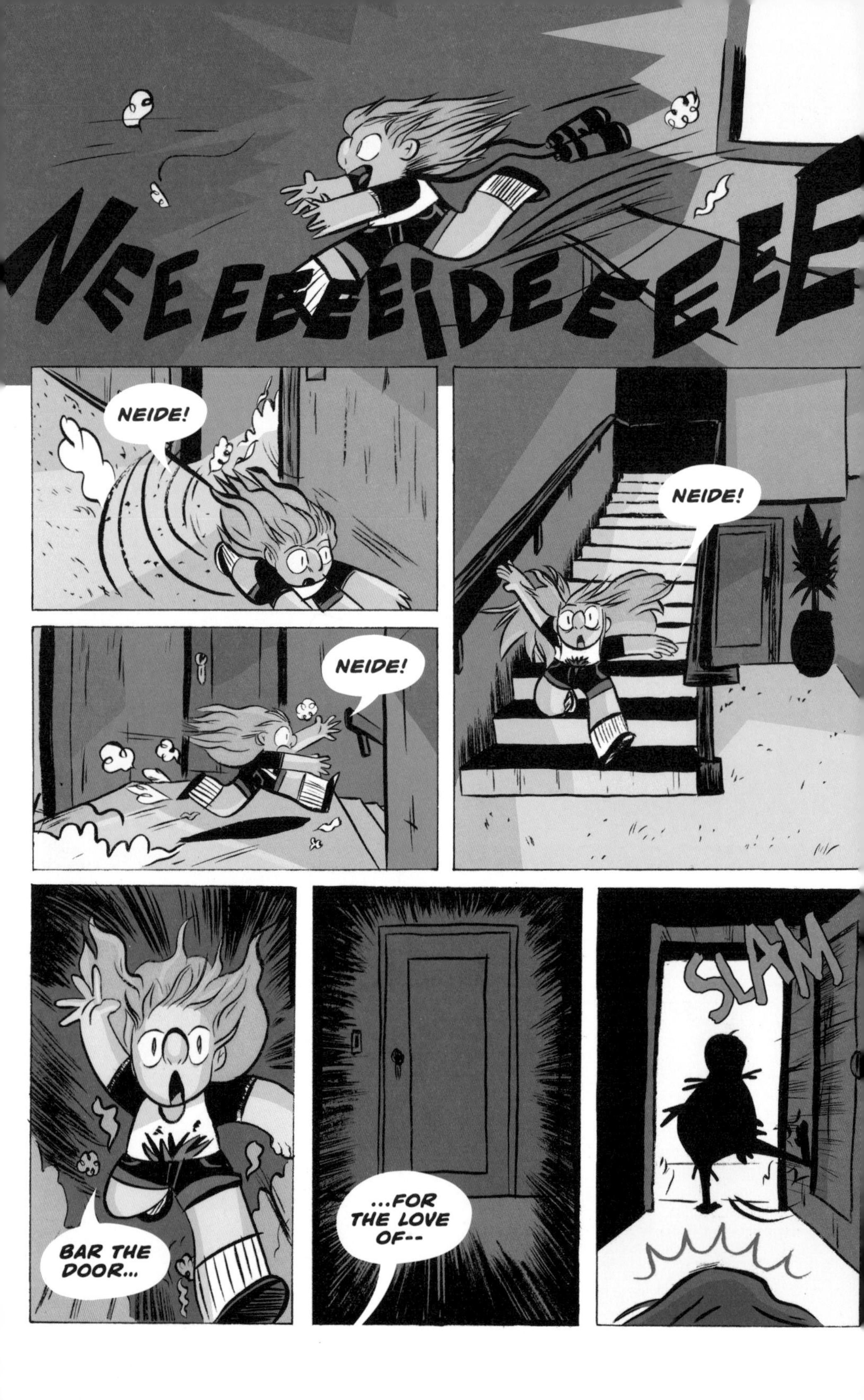
NEEEEEIDEEEEE
NEIDE!
NEIDE!
NEIDE!
BAR THE DOOR...
...FOR THE LOVE OF--
SLAM

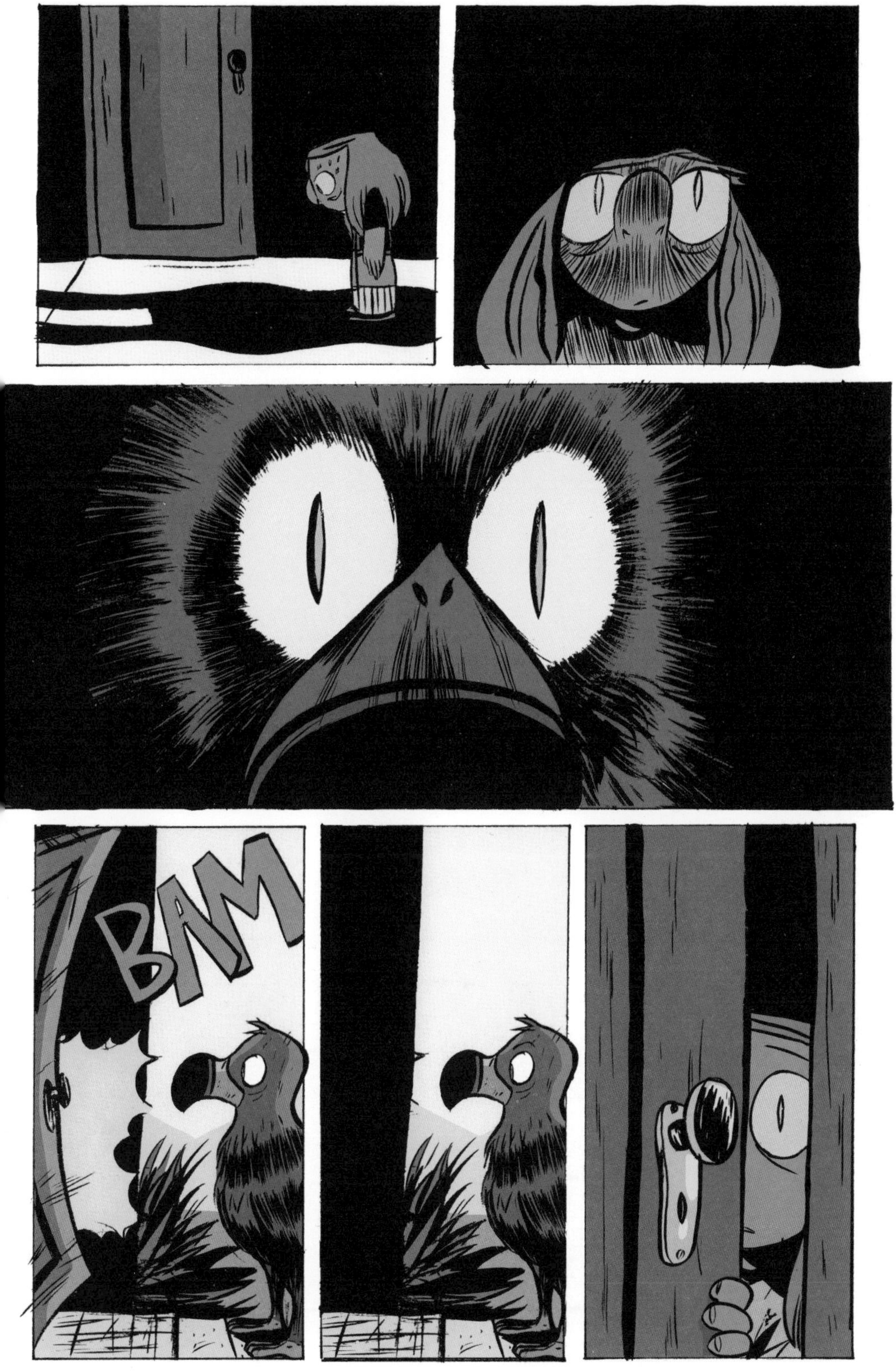
BAM

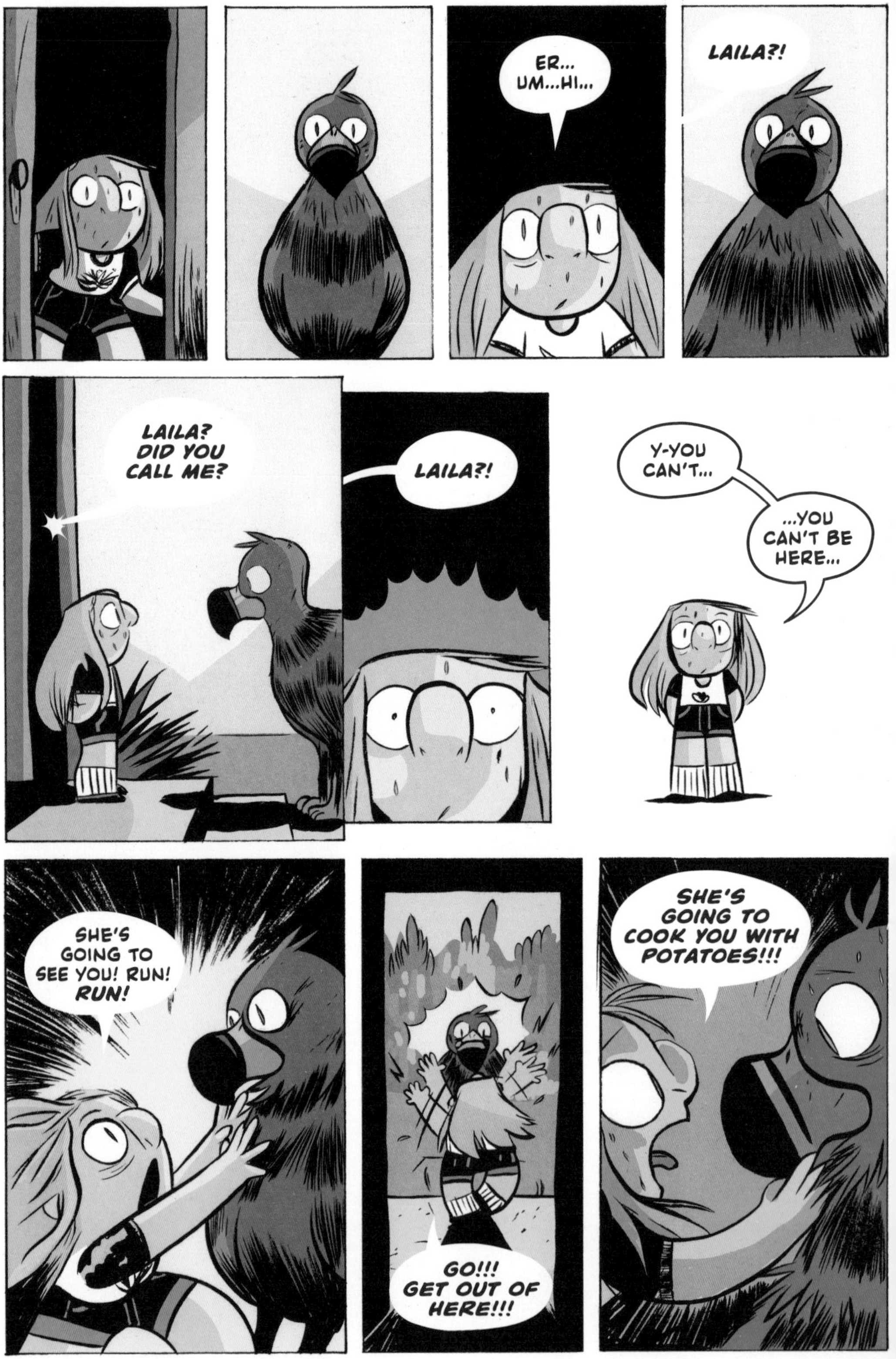
ER...
UM...HI...
LAILA?!
LAILA?
DID YOU
CALL ME?
LAILA?!
Y-YOU
CAN'T...
...YOU
CAN'T BE
HERE...
SHE'S
GOING TO
SEE YOU! RUN!
RUN!
GO!!!
GET OUT OF
HERE!!!
SHE'S
GOING TO
COOK YOU WITH
POTATOES!!!

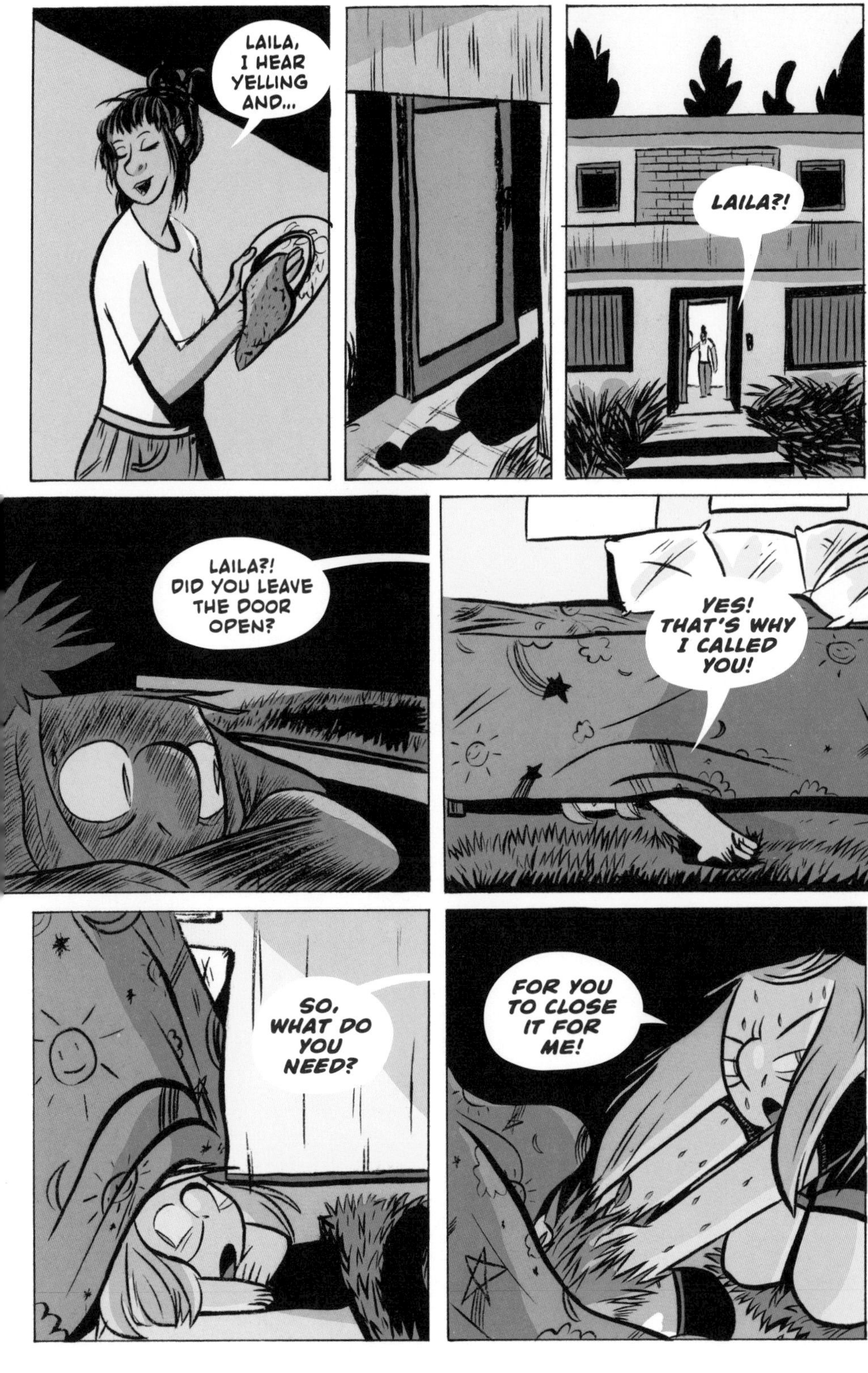
LAILA, I HEAR YELLING AND...
LAILA?!
LAILA?! DID YOU LEAVE THE DOOR OPEN?
YES! THAT'S WHY I CALLED YOU!
SO, WHAT DO YOU NEED?
FOR YOU TO CLOSE IT FOR ME!

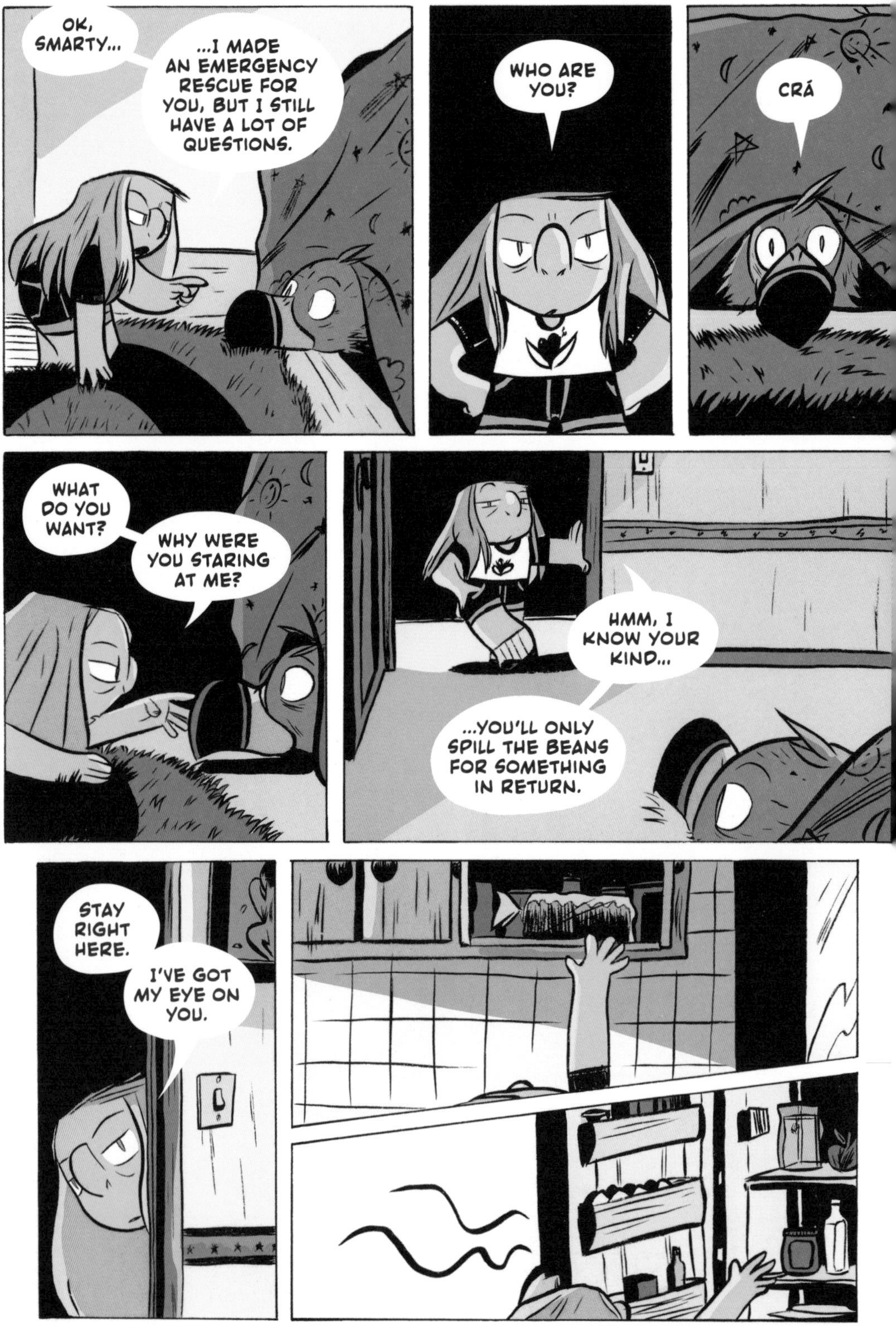
OK, SMARTY...
...I MADE AN EMERGENCY RESCUE FOR YOU, BUT I STILL HAVE A LOT OF QUESTIONS.
WHO ARE YOU?
CRÁ
WHAT DO YOU WANT?
WHY WERE YOU STARING AT ME?
HMM, I KNOW YOUR KIND...
...YOU'LL ONLY SPILL THE BEANS FOR SOMETHING IN RETURN.
STAY RIGHT HERE.
I'VE GOT MY EYE ON YOU.

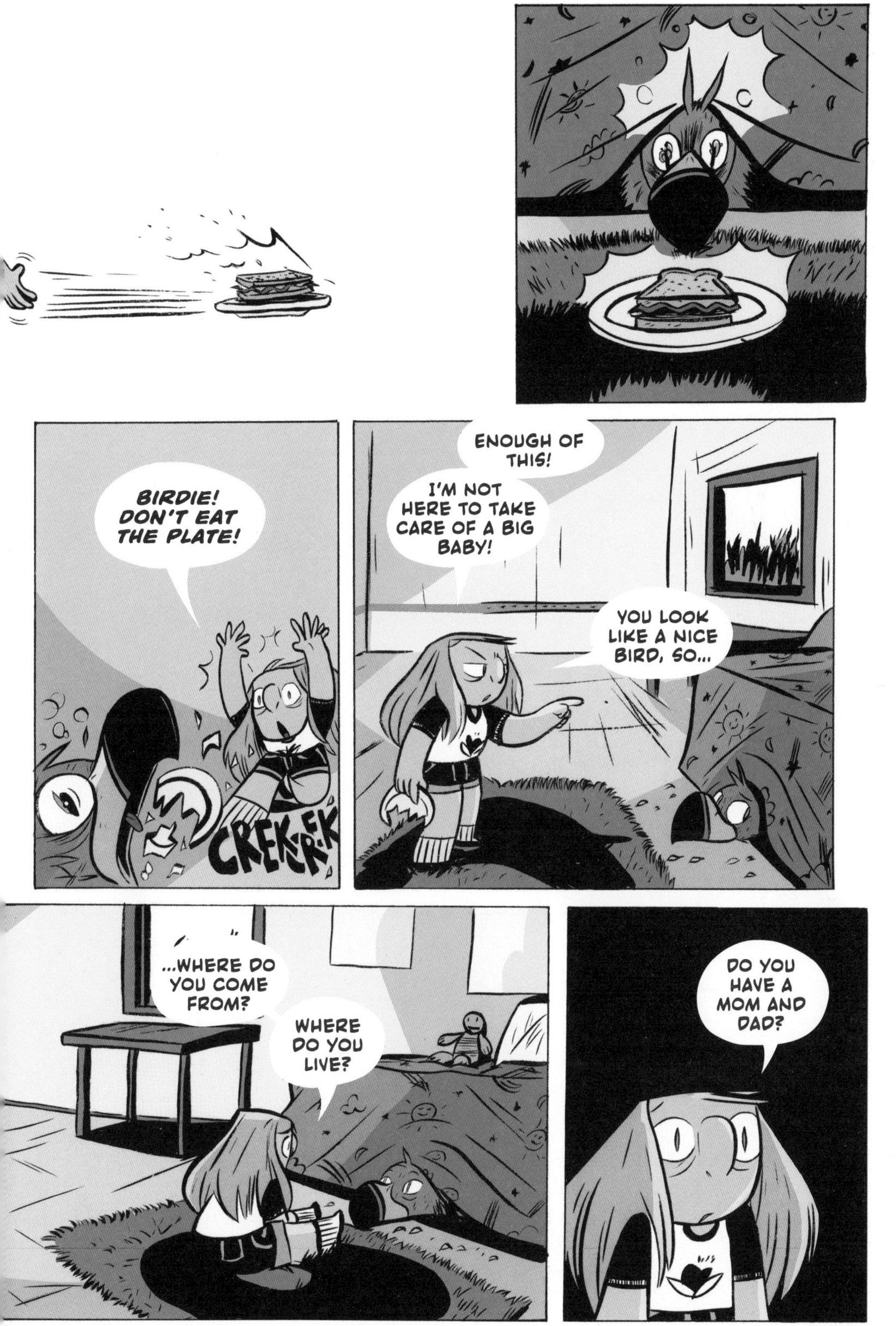
BIRDIE! DON'T EAT THE PLATE!
CREK-EK-CR-K
ENOUGH OF THIS!
I'M NOT HERE TO TAKE CARE OF A BIG BABY!
YOU LOOK LIKE A NICE BIRD, SO...
...WHERE DO YOU COME FROM?
WHERE DO YOU LIVE?
DO YOU HAVE A MOM AND DAD?

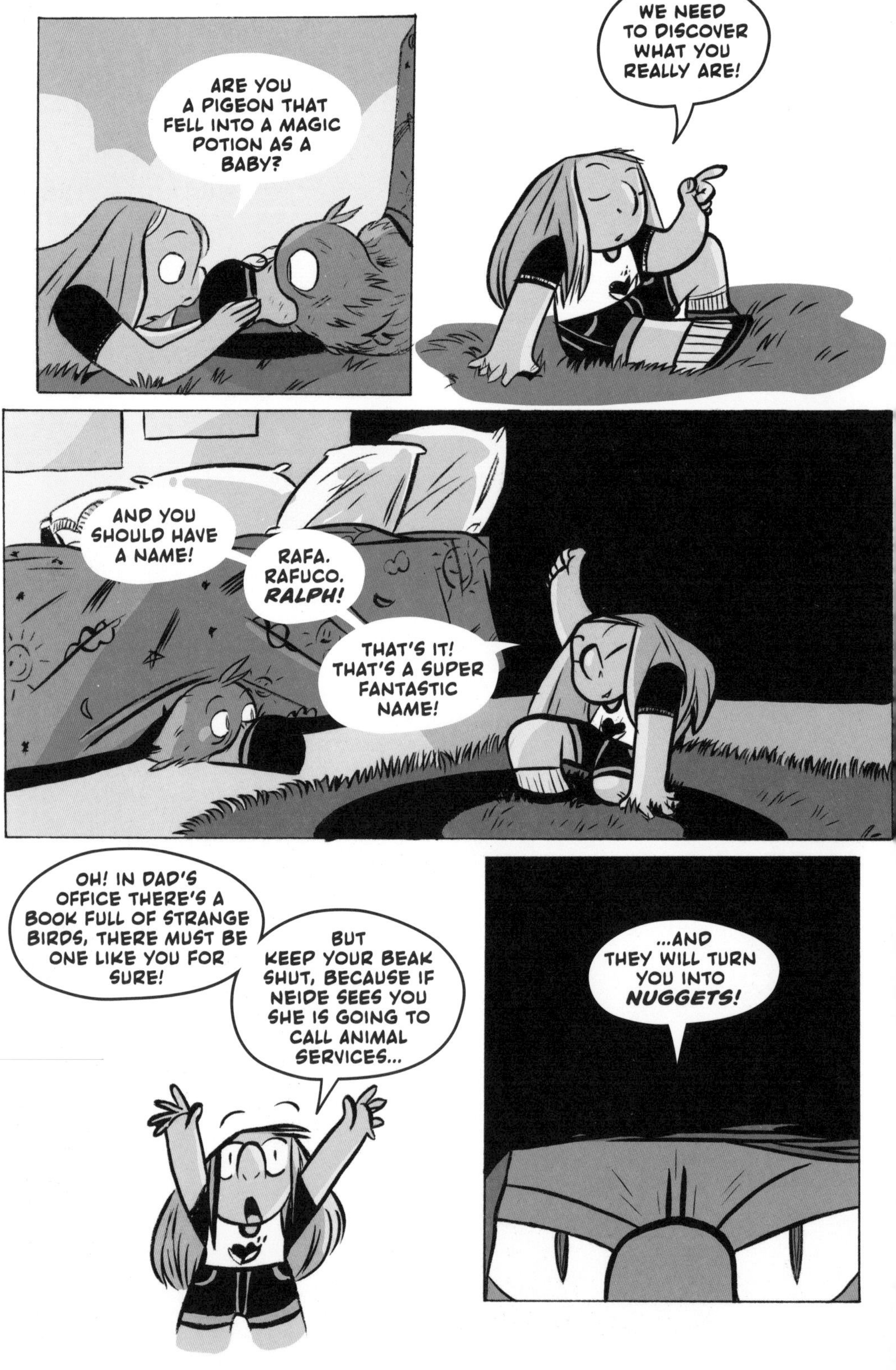
ARE YOU A PIGEON THAT FELL INTO A MAGIC POTION AS A BABY?
WE NEED TO DISCOVER WHAT YOU REALLY ARE!
AND YOU SHOULD HAVE A NAME!
RAFA. RAFUCO. *RALPH!*
THAT'S IT! THAT'S A SUPER FANTASTIC NAME!
OH! IN DAD'S OFFICE THERE'S A BOOK FULL OF STRANGE BIRDS, THERE MUST BE ONE LIKE YOU FOR SURE!
BUT KEEP YOUR BEAK SHUT, BECAUSE IF NEIDE SEES YOU SHE IS GOING TO CALL ANIMAL SERVICES...
...AND THEY WILL TURN YOU INTO *NUGGETS!*

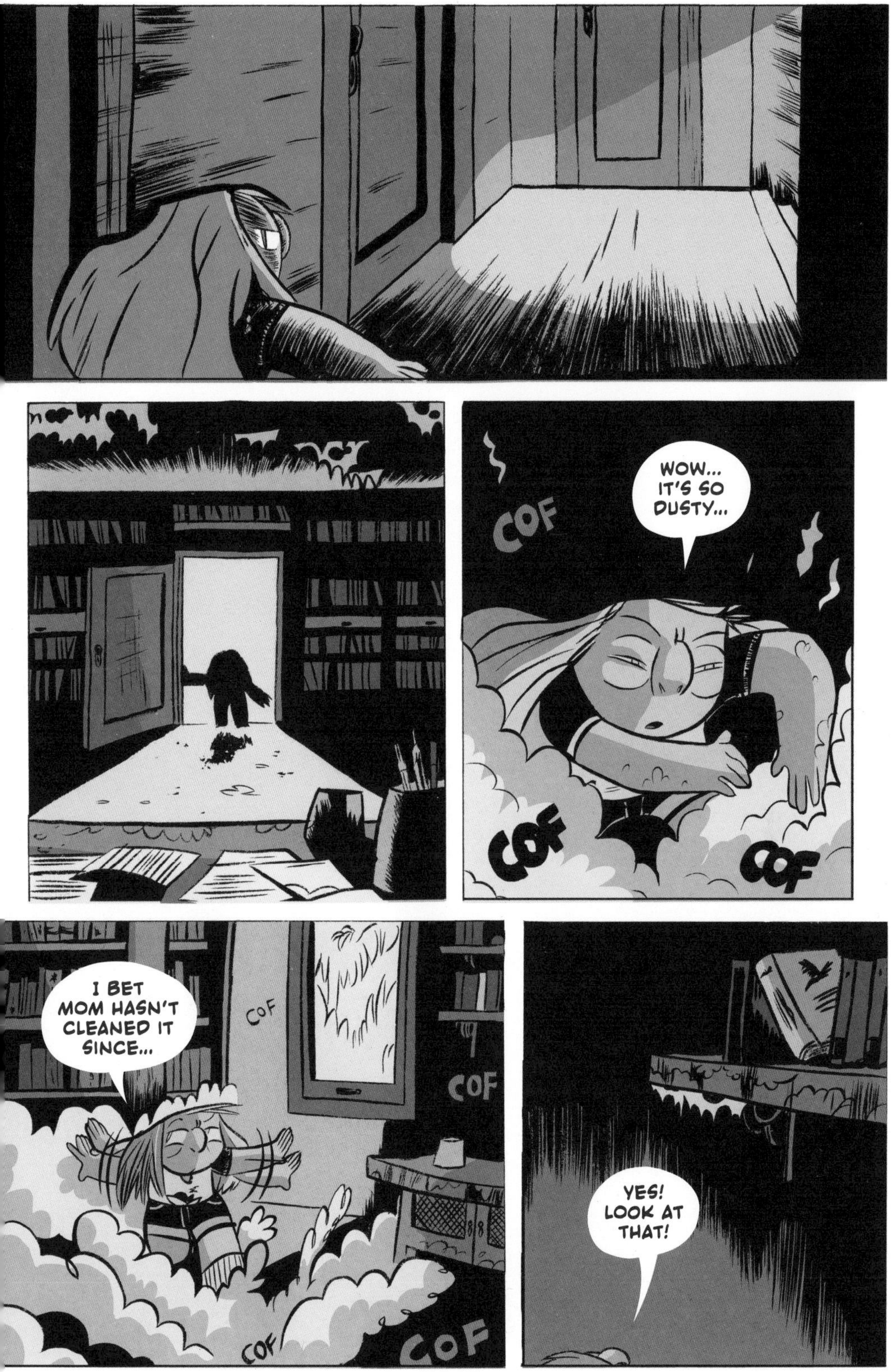
WOW... IT'S SO DUSTY...
COF
COF
COF
I BET MOM HASN'T CLEANED IT SINCE...
COF
COF
COF
COF
YES! LOOK AT THAT!

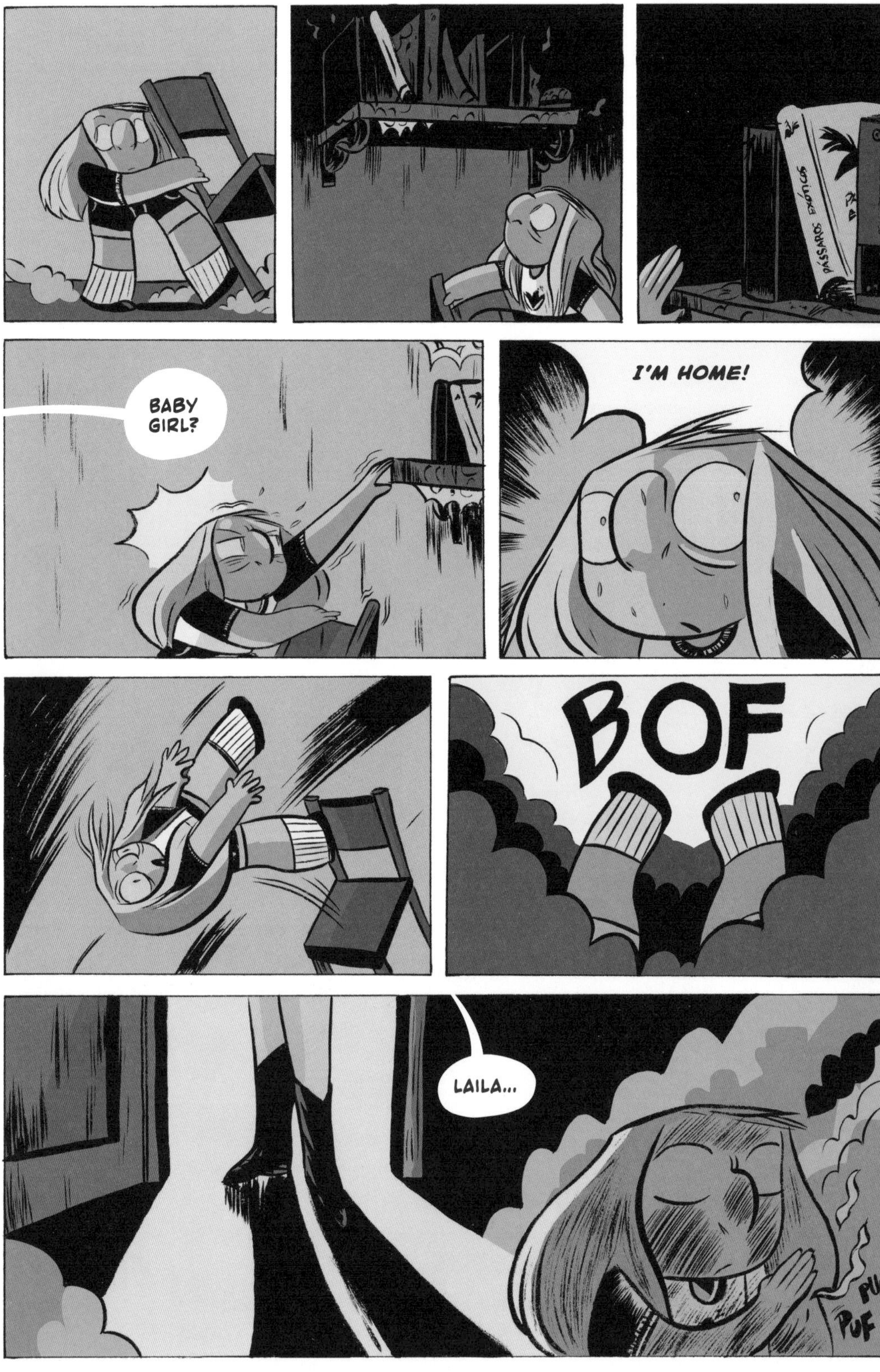
PÁSSAROS EXÓTICOS
BABY GIRL?
I'M HOME!
BOF
LAILA...
PUF
PUF

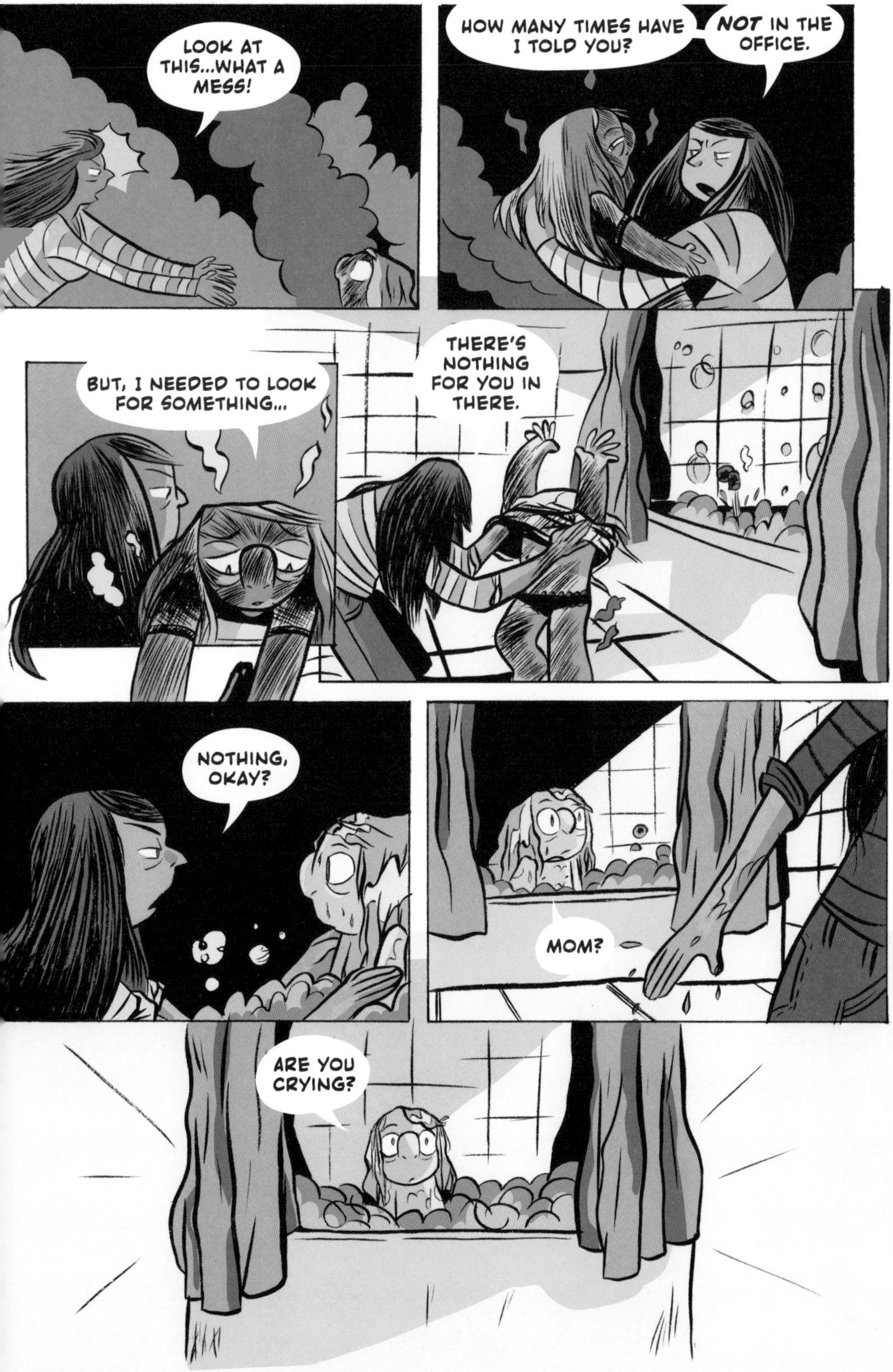
LOOK AT THIS...WHAT A MESS!
HOW MANY TIMES HAVE I TOLD YOU?
NOT IN THE OFFICE.
BUT, I NEEDED TO LOOK FOR SOMETHING...
THERE'S NOTHING FOR YOU IN THERE.
NOTHING, OKAY?
MOM?
ARE YOU CRYING?

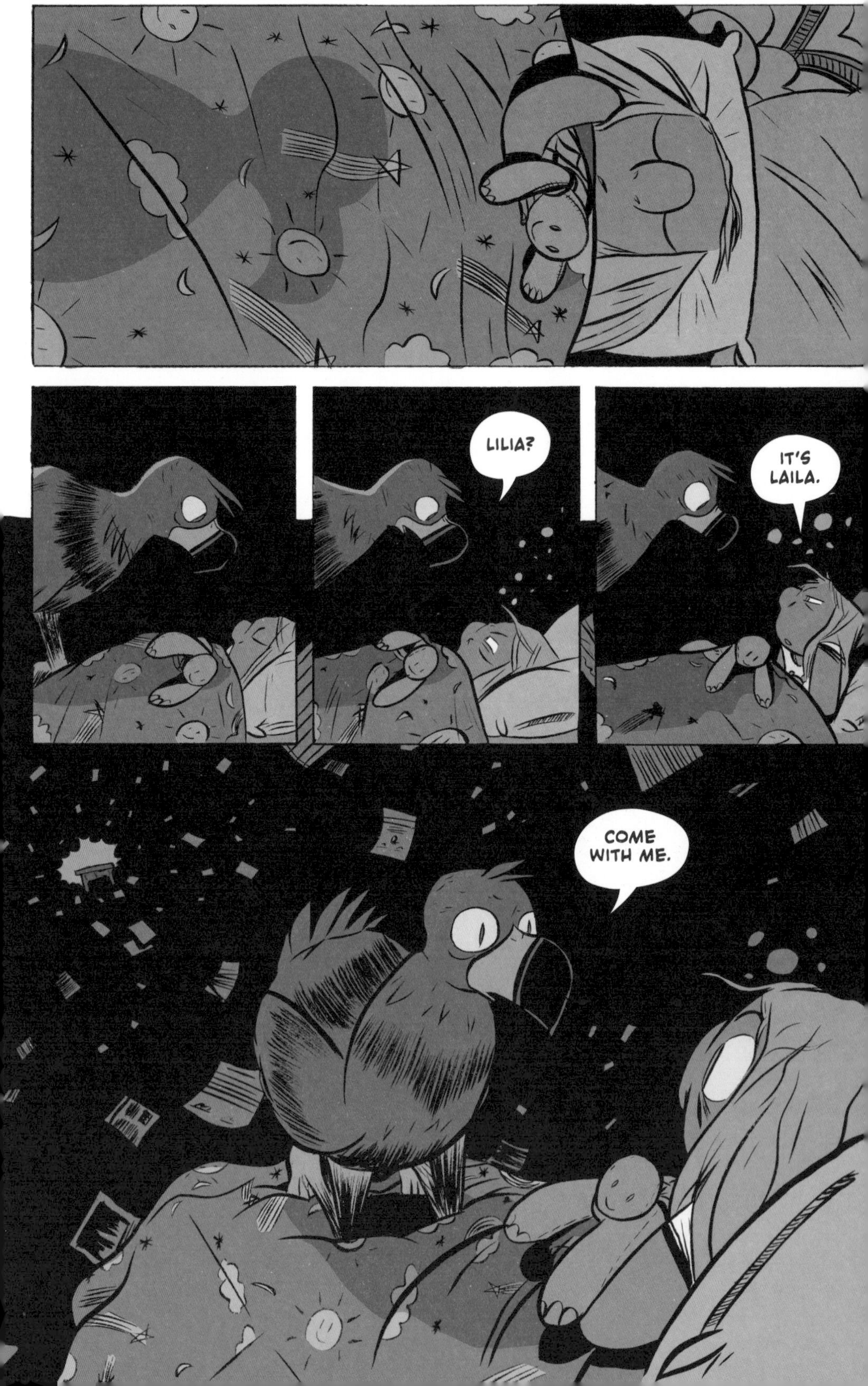
LILIA?
IT'S LAILA.
COME WITH ME.

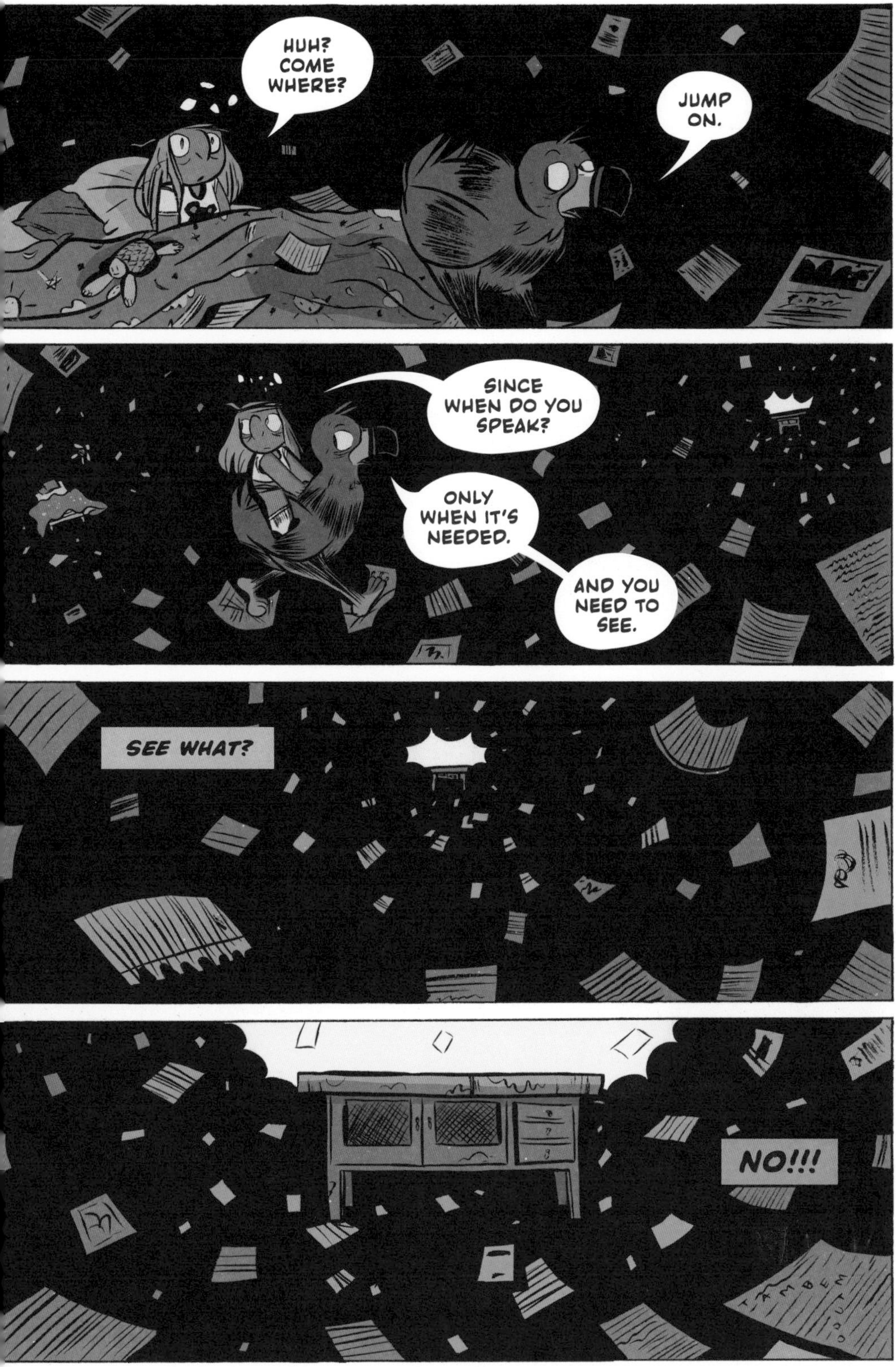
HUH? COME WHERE?
JUMP ON.
SINCE WHEN DO YOU SPEAK?
ONLY WHEN IT'S NEEDED.
AND YOU NEED TO SEE.
SEE WHAT?
NO!!!

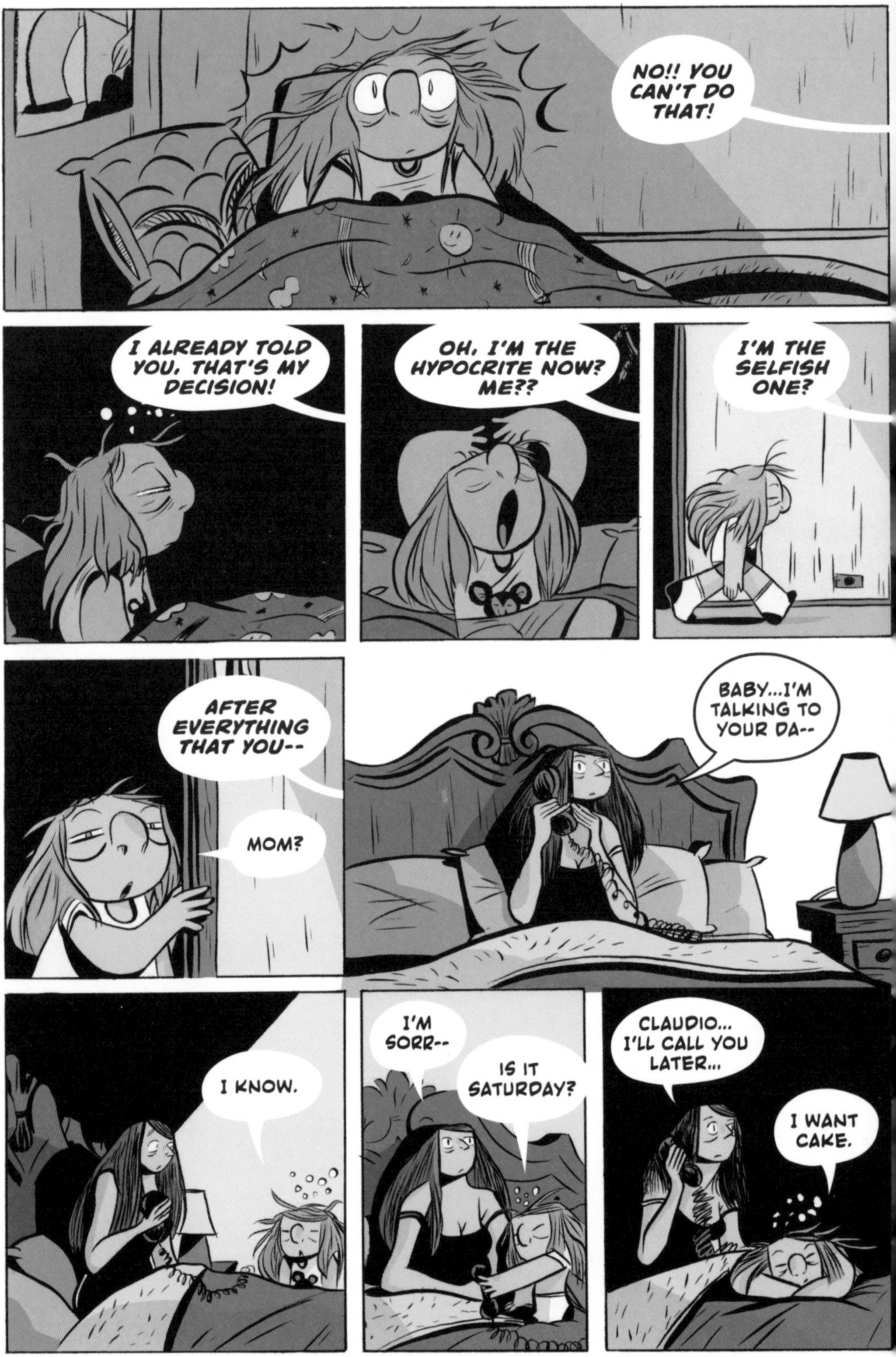
NO!! YOU CAN'T DO THAT!
I ALREADY TOLD YOU, THAT'S MY DECISION!
OH, I'M THE HYPOCRITE NOW? ME??
I'M THE SELFISH ONE?
AFTER EVERYTHING THAT YOU--
MOM?
BABY...I'M TALKING TO YOUR DA--
I KNOW.
I'M SORR--
IS IT SATURDAY?
CLAUDIO... I'LL CALL YOU LATER...
I WANT CAKE.

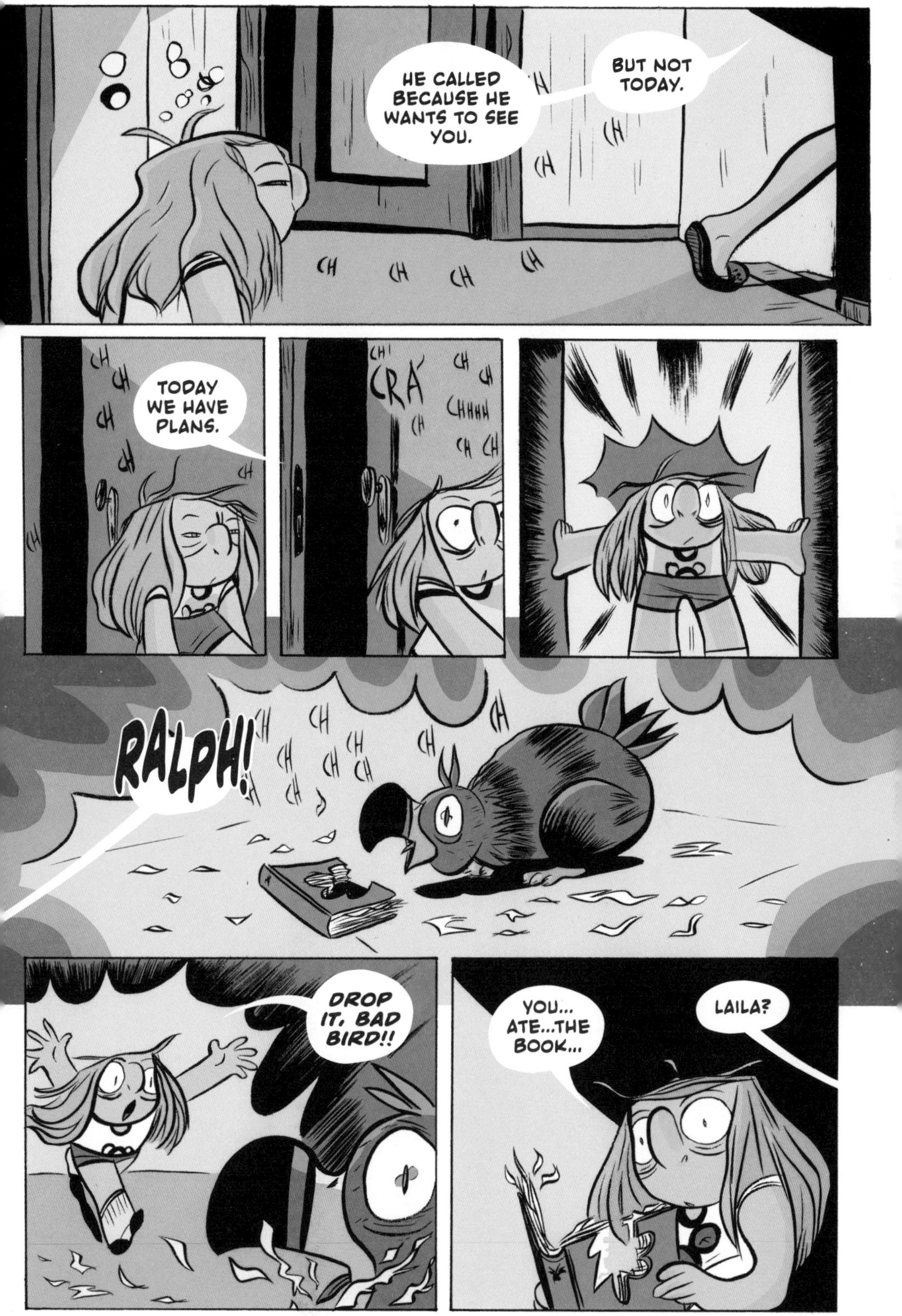
HE CALLED BECAUSE HE WANTS TO SEE YOU.
BUT NOT TODAY.
CH CH CH CH CH CH CH
TODAY WE HAVE PLANS.
CH CH CH CH CH CH
CH CRÁ CH CH CHHHH CH CH CH
RALPH!
CH CH CH CH CH CH CH CH CH
DROP IT, BAD BIRD!!
YOU... ATE...THE BOOK...
LAILA?

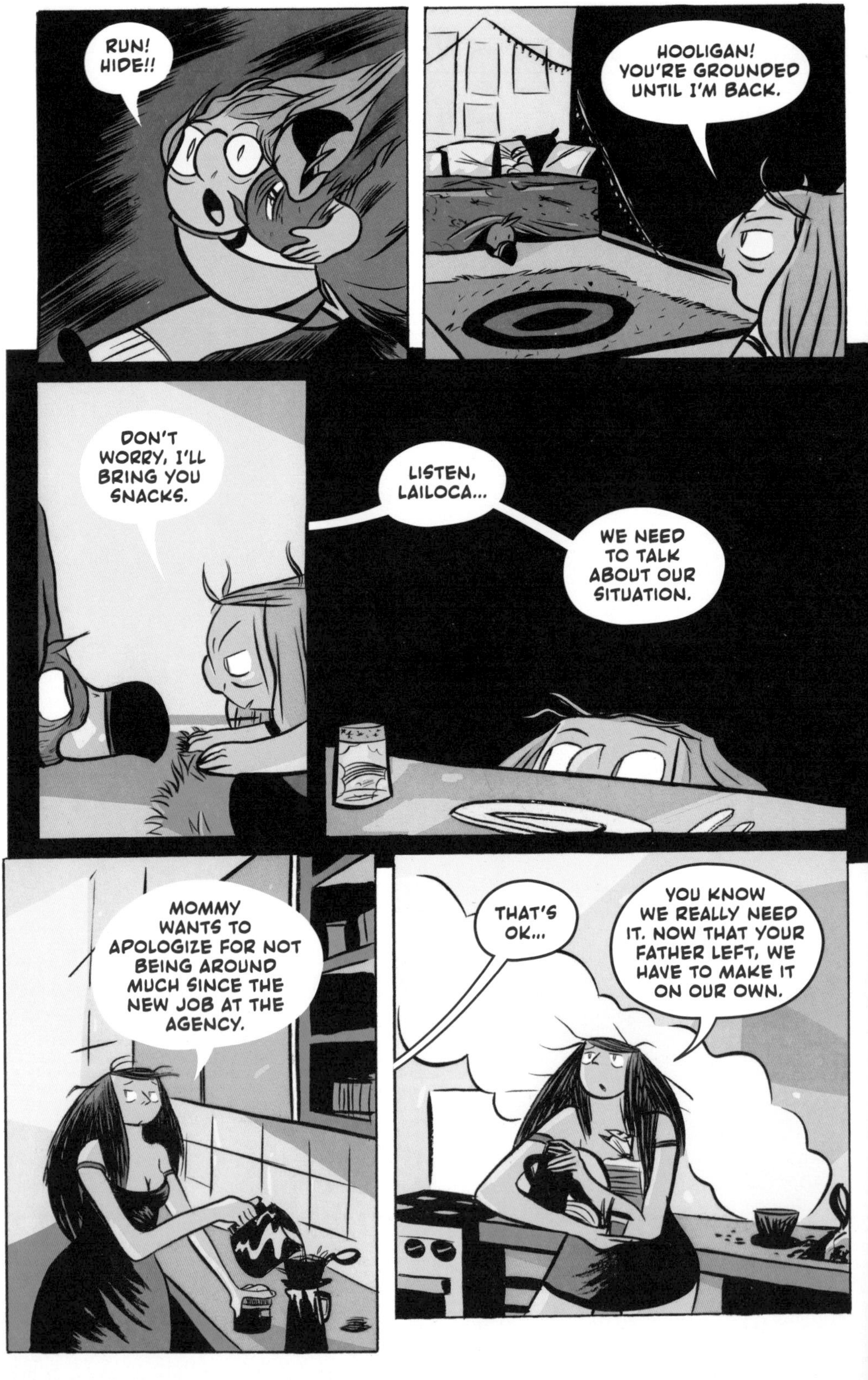
RUN! HIDE!!
HOOLIGAN! YOU'RE GROUNDED UNTIL I'M BACK.
DON'T WORRY, I'LL BRING YOU SNACKS.
LISTEN, LAILOCA...
WE NEED TO TALK ABOUT OUR SITUATION.
MOMMY WANTS TO APOLOGIZE FOR NOT BEING AROUND MUCH SINCE THE NEW JOB AT THE AGENCY.
THAT'S OK...
YOU KNOW WE REALLY NEED IT. NOW THAT YOUR FATHER LEFT, WE HAVE TO MAKE IT ON OUR OWN.

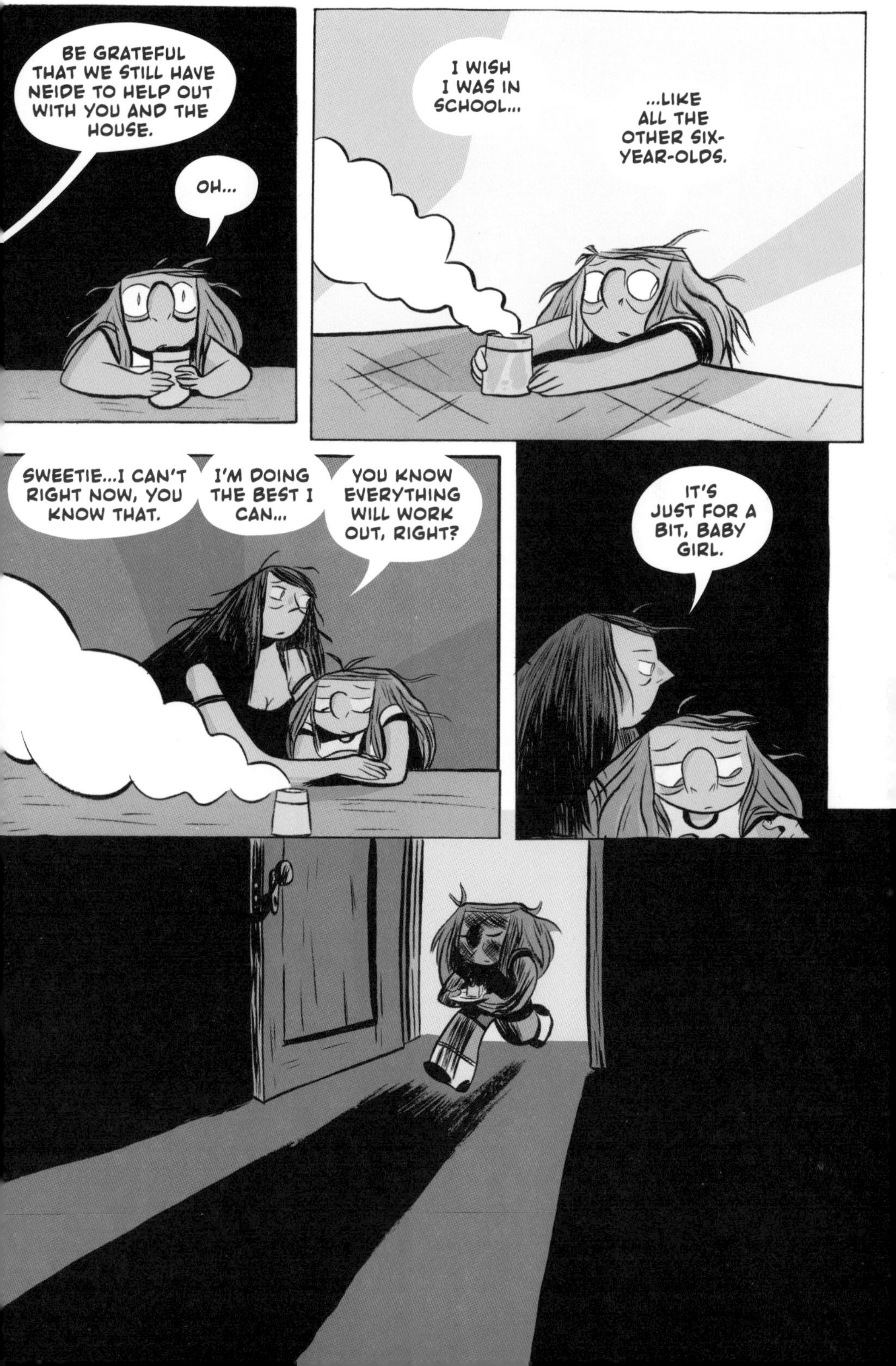

BE GRATEFUL THAT WE STILL HAVE NEIDE TO HELP OUT WITH YOU AND THE HOUSE.
OH...
I WISH I WAS IN SCHOOL...
...LIKE ALL THE OTHER SIX-YEAR-OLDS.
SWEETIE...I CAN'T RIGHT NOW, YOU KNOW THAT.
I'M DOING THE BEST I CAN...
YOU KNOW EVERYTHING WILL WORK OUT, RIGHT?
IT'S JUST FOR A BIT, BABY GIRL.

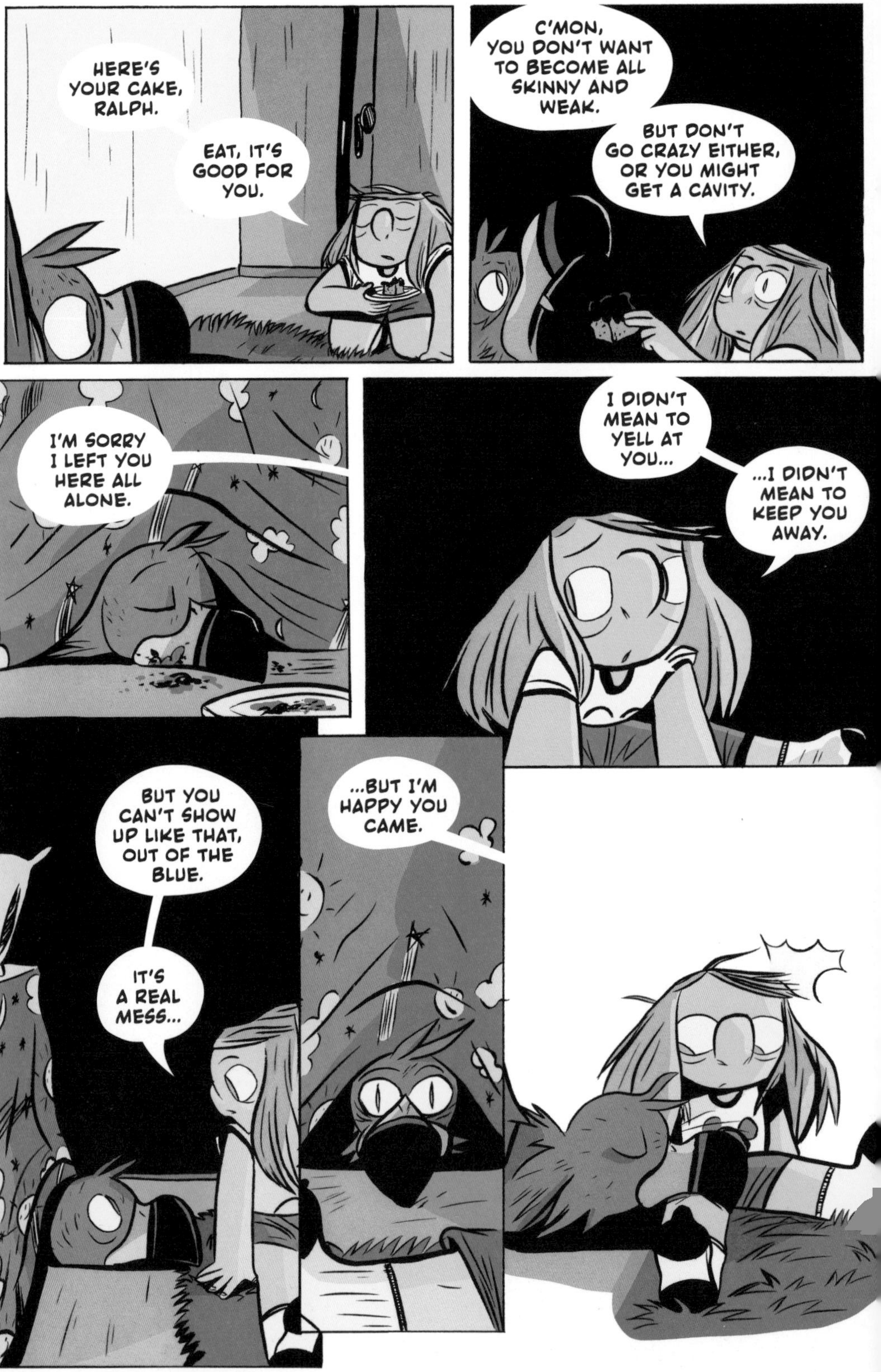
HERE'S YOUR CAKE, RALPH.
EAT, IT'S GOOD FOR YOU.
C'MON, YOU DON'T WANT TO BECOME ALL SKINNY AND WEAK.
BUT DON'T GO CRAZY EITHER, OR YOU MIGHT GET A CAVITY.
I'M SORRY I LEFT YOU HERE ALL ALONE.
I DIDN'T MEAN TO YELL AT YOU...
...I DIDN'T MEAN TO KEEP YOU AWAY.
BUT YOU CAN'T SHOW UP LIKE THAT, OUT OF THE BLUE.
IT'S A REAL MESS...
...BUT I'M HAPPY YOU CAME.

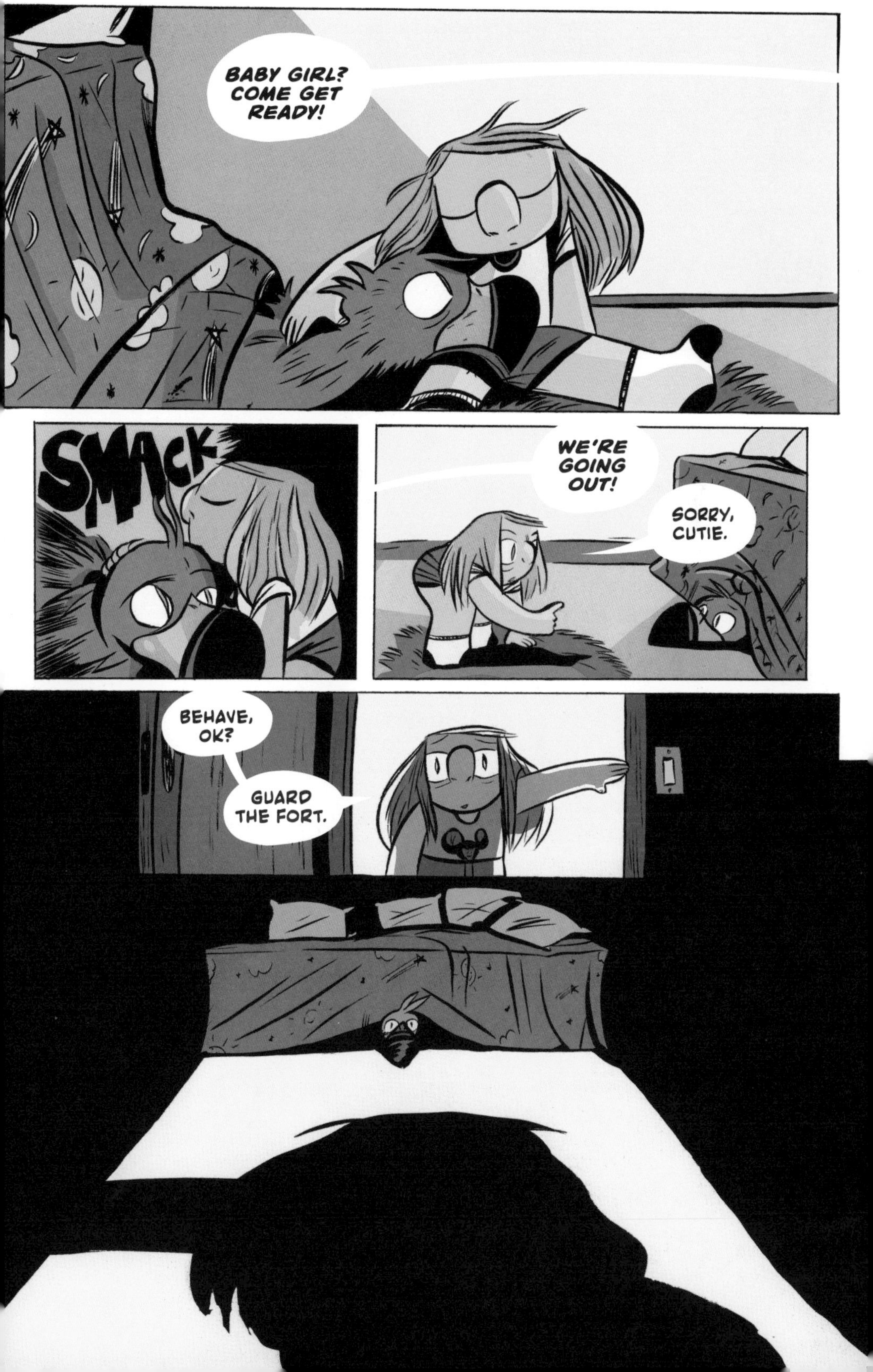
BABY GIRL? COME GET READY!
SMACK
WE'RE GOING OUT!
SORRY, CUTIE.
BEHAVE, OK?
GUARD THE FORT.

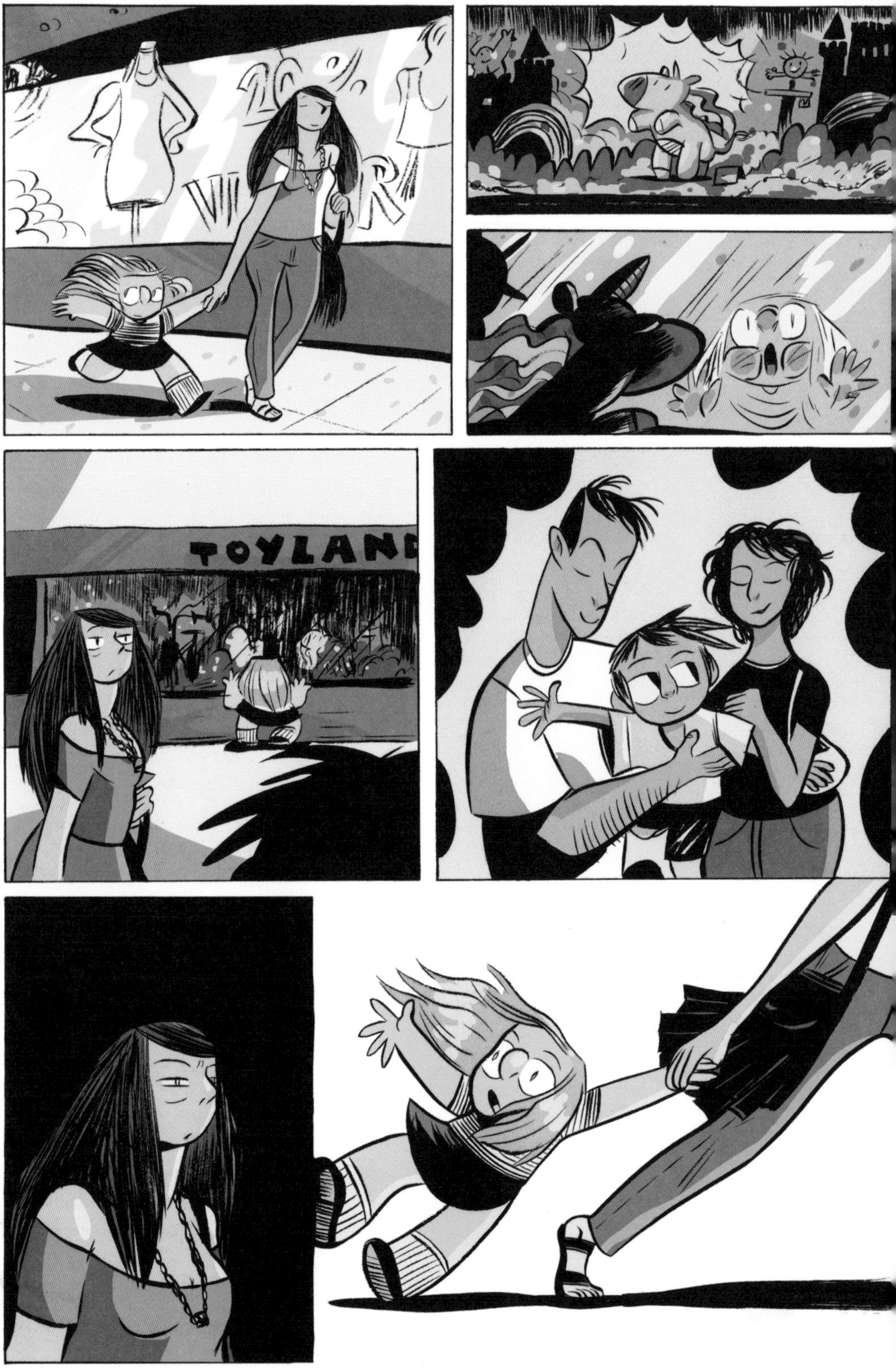
TOYLAND

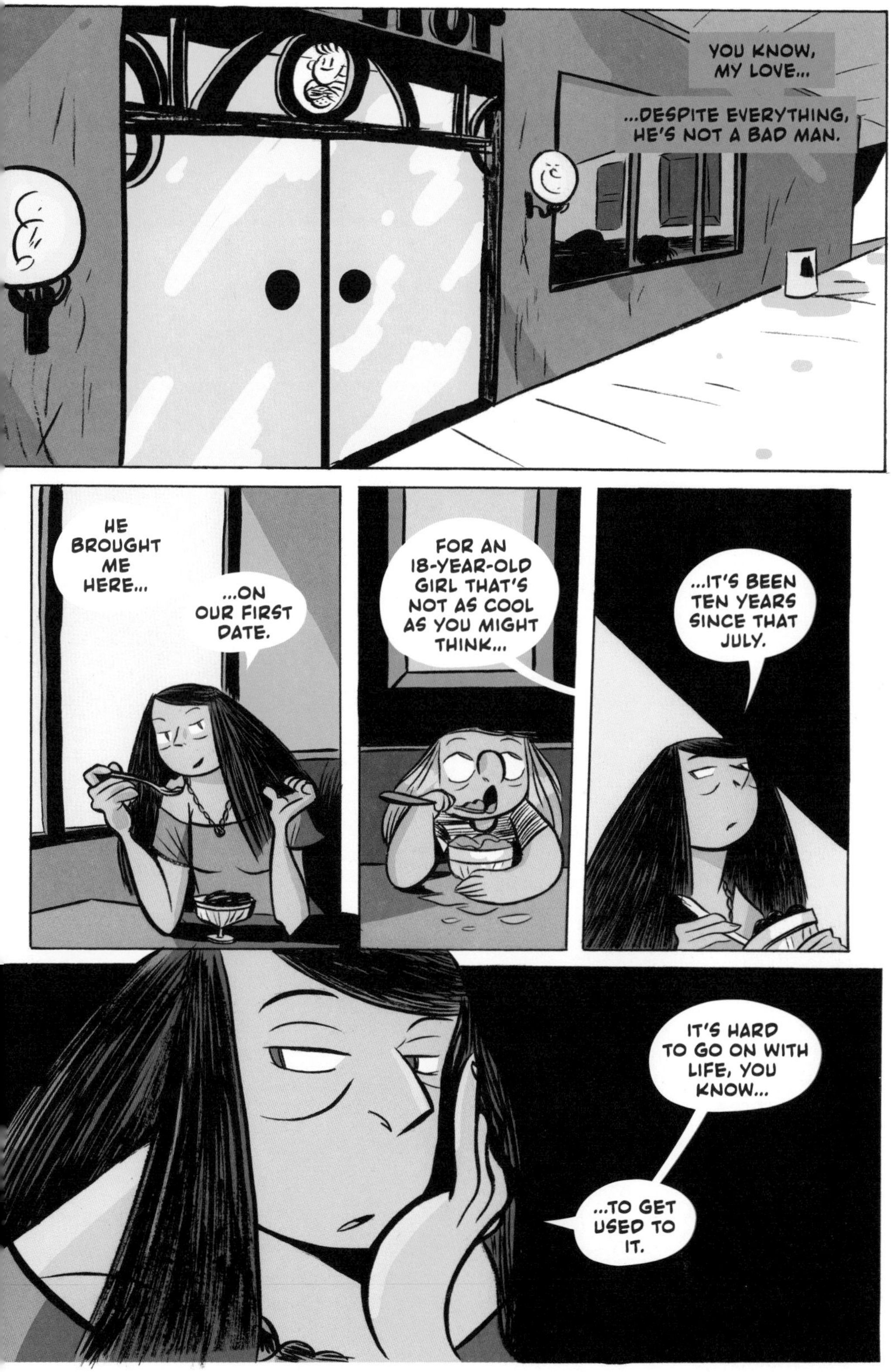
YOU KNOW, MY LOVE...
...DESPITE EVERYTHING, HE'S NOT A BAD MAN.
HE BROUGHT ME HERE...
...ON OUR FIRST DATE.
FOR AN 18-YEAR-OLD GIRL THAT'S NOT AS COOL AS YOU MIGHT THINK...
...IT'S BEEN TEN YEARS SINCE THAT JULY.
IT'S HARD TO GO ON WITH LIFE, YOU KNOW...
...TO GET USED TO IT.

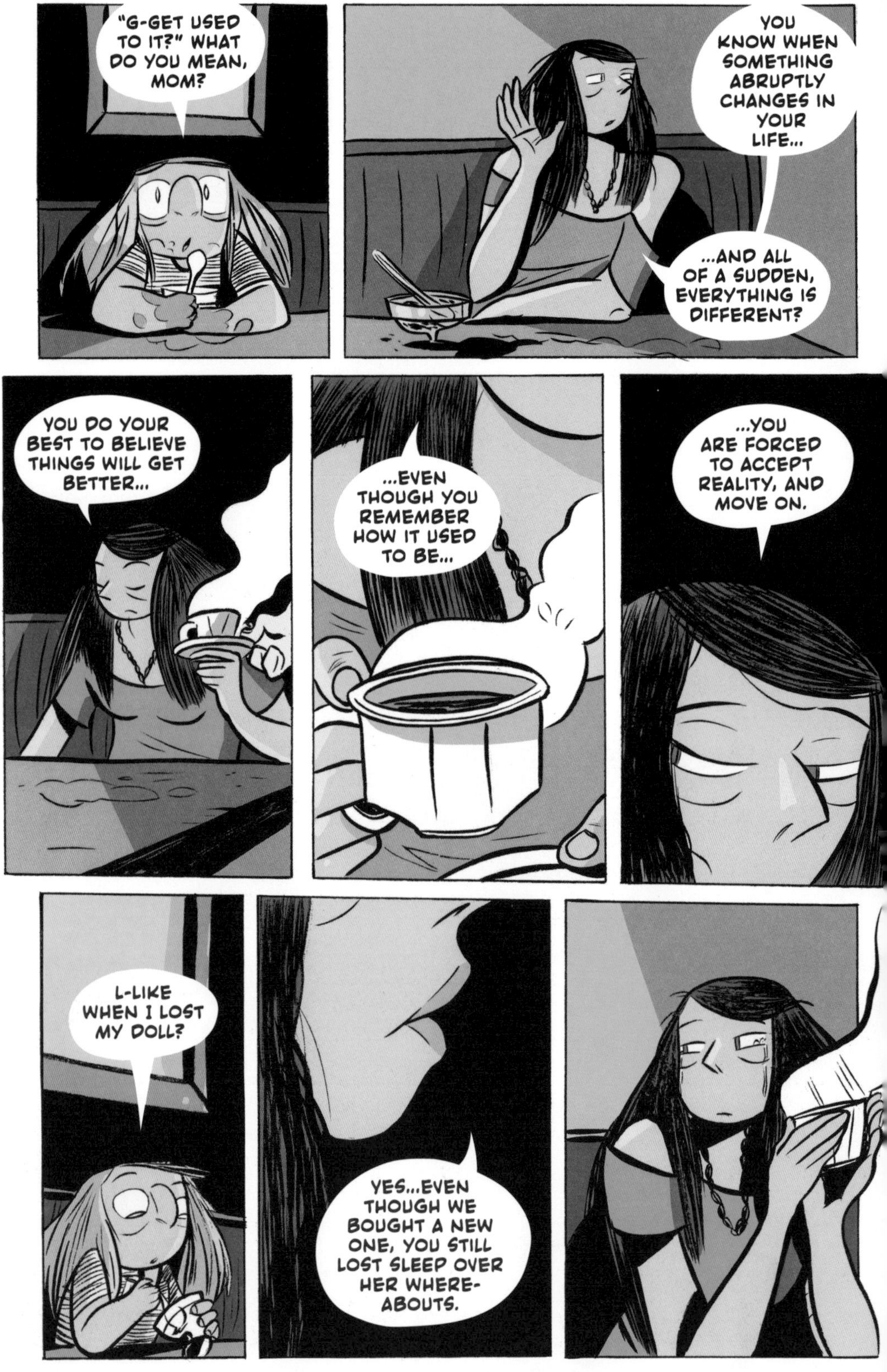
"G-GET USED TO IT?" WHAT DO YOU MEAN, MOM?
YOU KNOW WHEN SOMETHING ABRUPTLY CHANGES IN YOUR LIFE...
...AND ALL OF A SUDDEN, EVERYTHING IS DIFFERENT?
YOU DO YOUR BEST TO BELIEVE THINGS WILL GET BETTER...
...EVEN THOUGH YOU REMEMBER HOW IT USED TO BE...
...YOU ARE FORCED TO ACCEPT REALITY, AND MOVE ON.
L-LIKE WHEN I LOST MY DOLL?
YES...EVEN THOUGH WE BOUGHT A NEW ONE, YOU STILL LOST SLEEP OVER HER WHERE-ABOUTS.

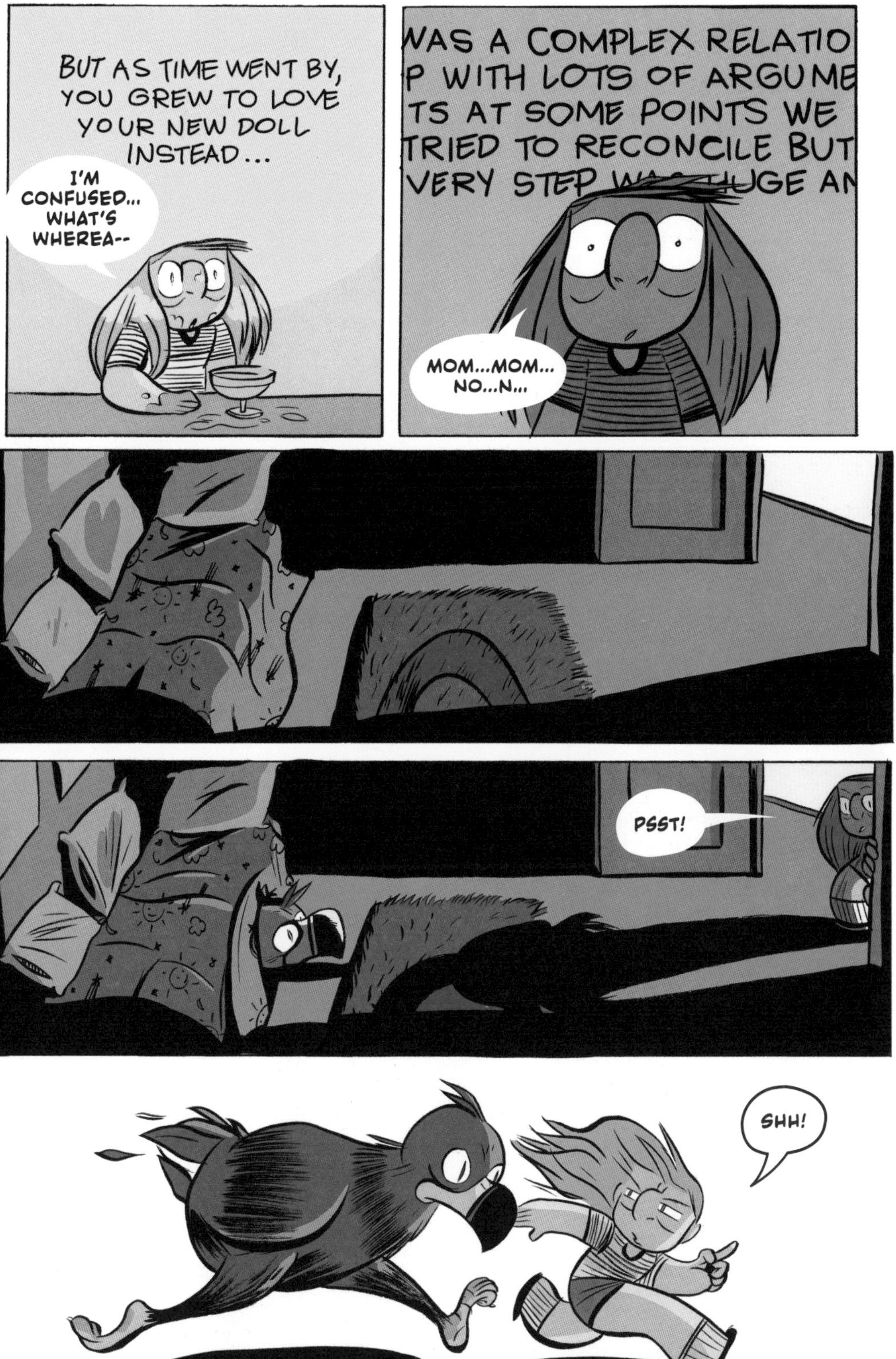
BUT AS TIME WENT BY, YOU GREW TO LOVE YOUR NEW DOLL INSTEAD...
I'M CONFUSED... WHAT'S WHEREA--
WAS A COMPLEX RELATIO
P WITH LOTS OF ARGUME
TS AT SOME POINTS WE
TRIED TO RECONCILE BUT
VERY STEP
UGE AN
MOM...MOM... NO...N...
PSST!
SHH!

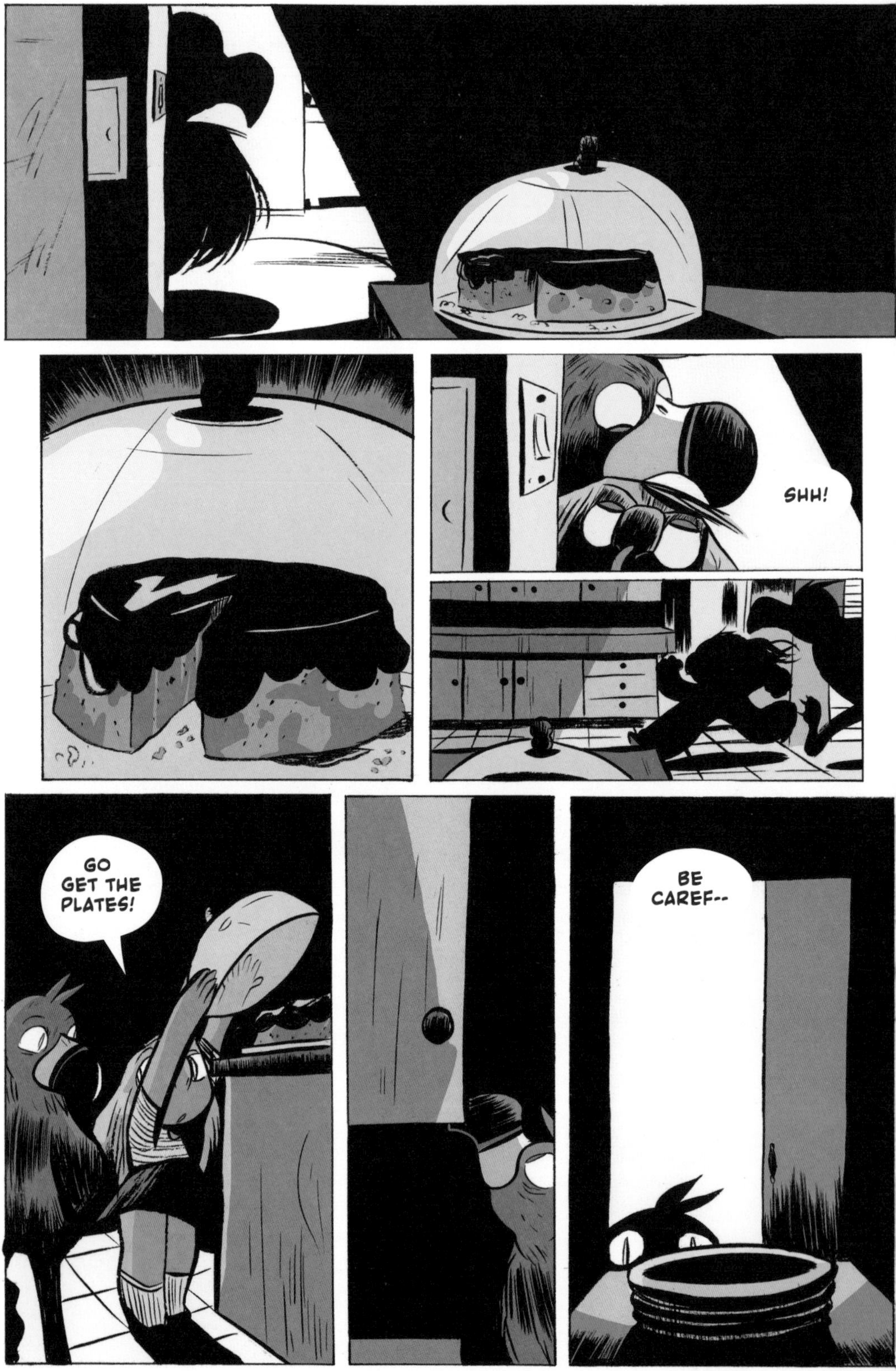
SHH!
GO GET THE PLATES!
BE CAREF--

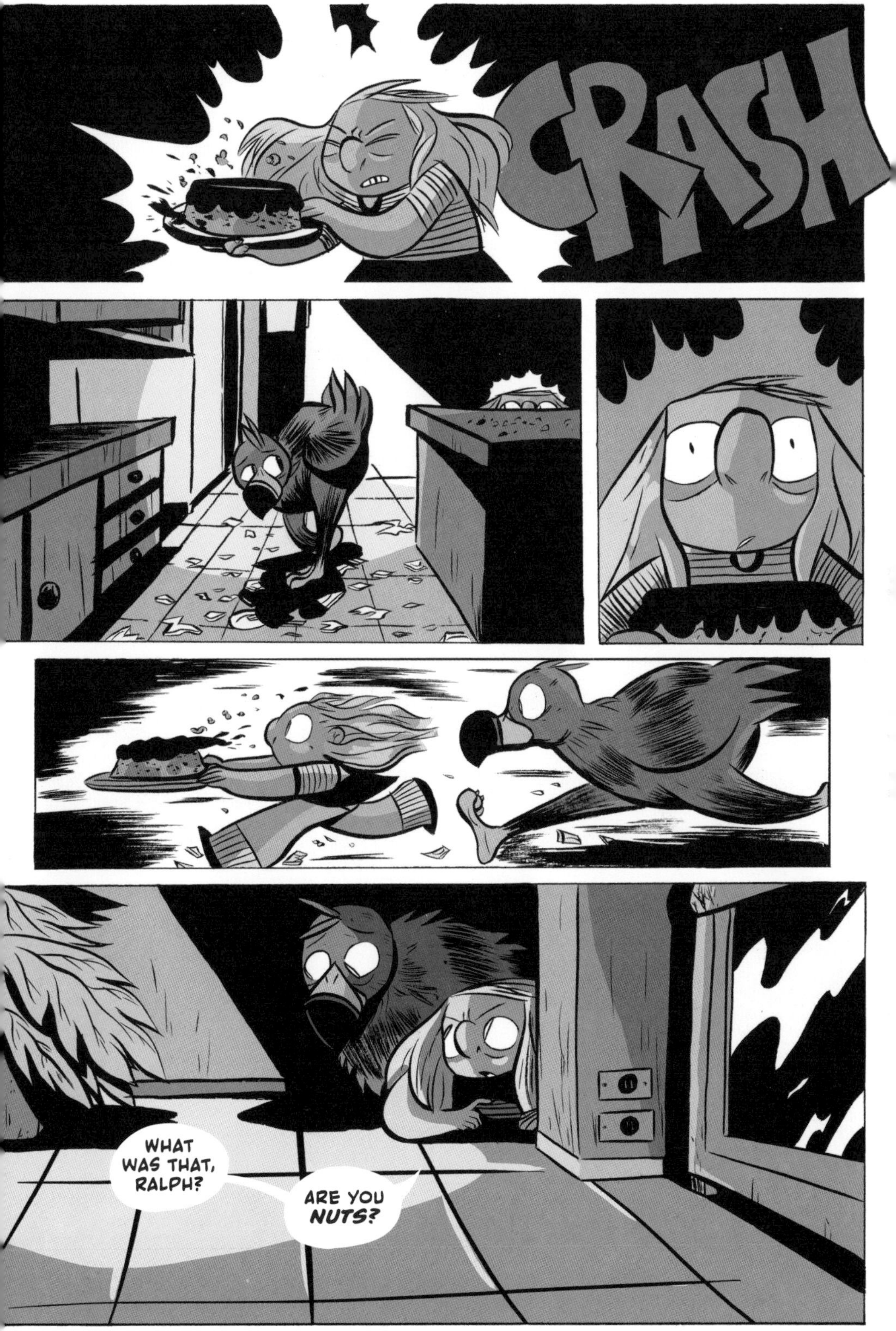
CRASH
WHAT WAS THAT, RALPH?
ARE YOU NUTS?

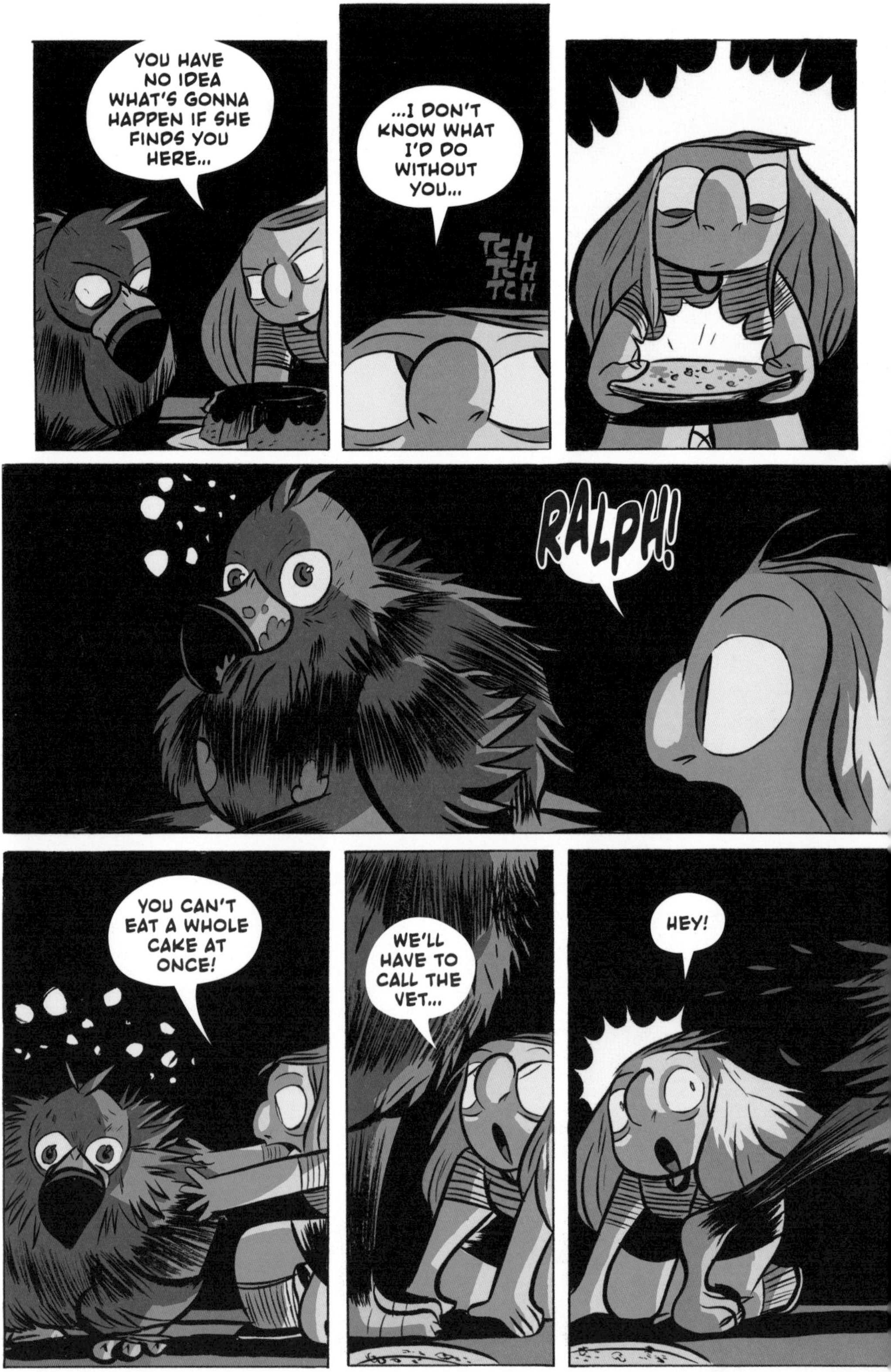
YOU HAVE NO IDEA WHAT'S GONNA HAPPEN IF SHE FINDS YOU HERE...
...I DON'T KNOW WHAT I'D DO WITHOUT YOU...
TCH TCH TCH
RALPH!
YOU CAN'T EAT A WHOLE CAKE AT ONCE!
WE'LL HAVE TO CALL THE VET...
HEY!

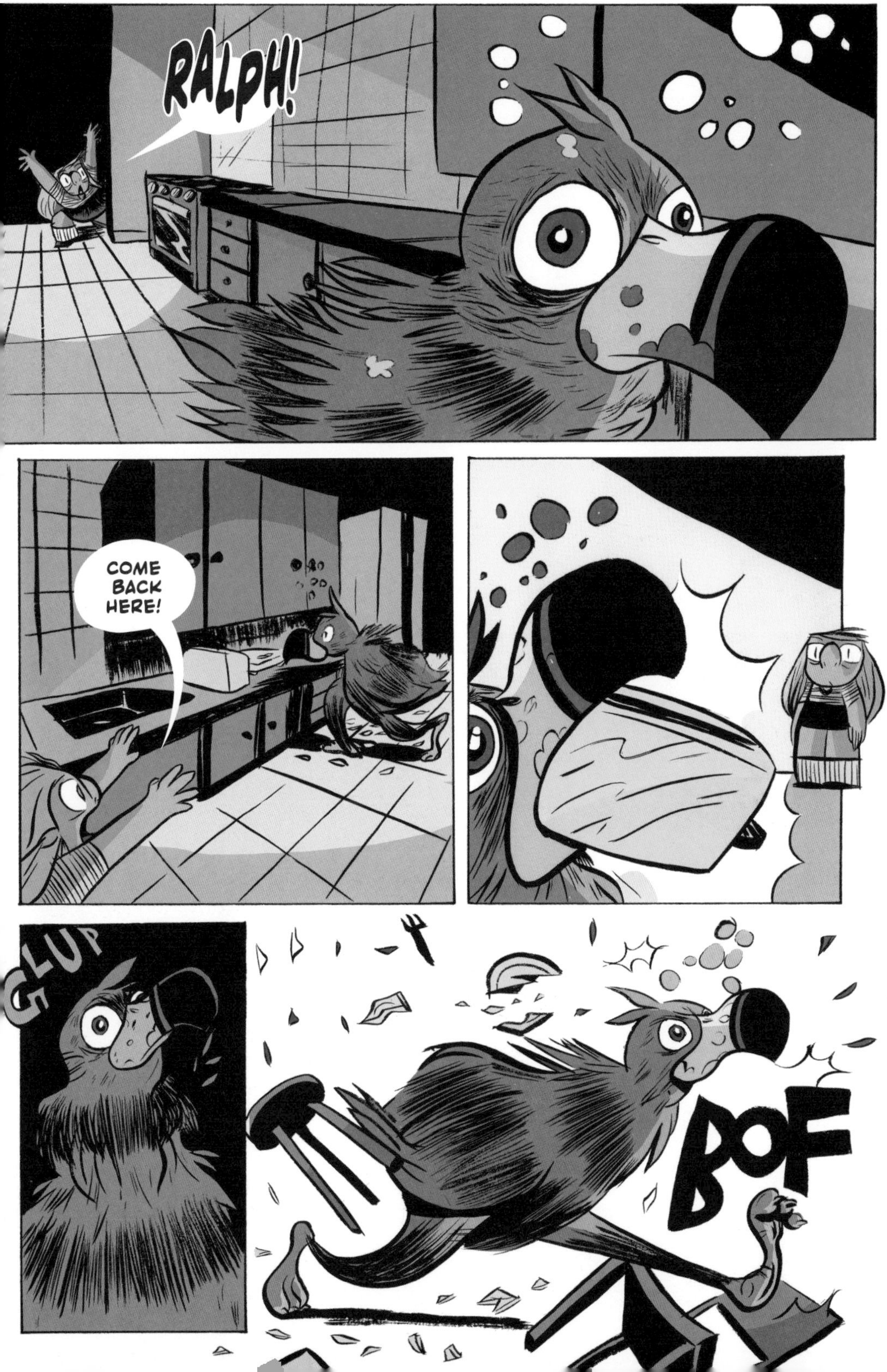
RALPH!
COME BACK HERE!
GLUP
BOF

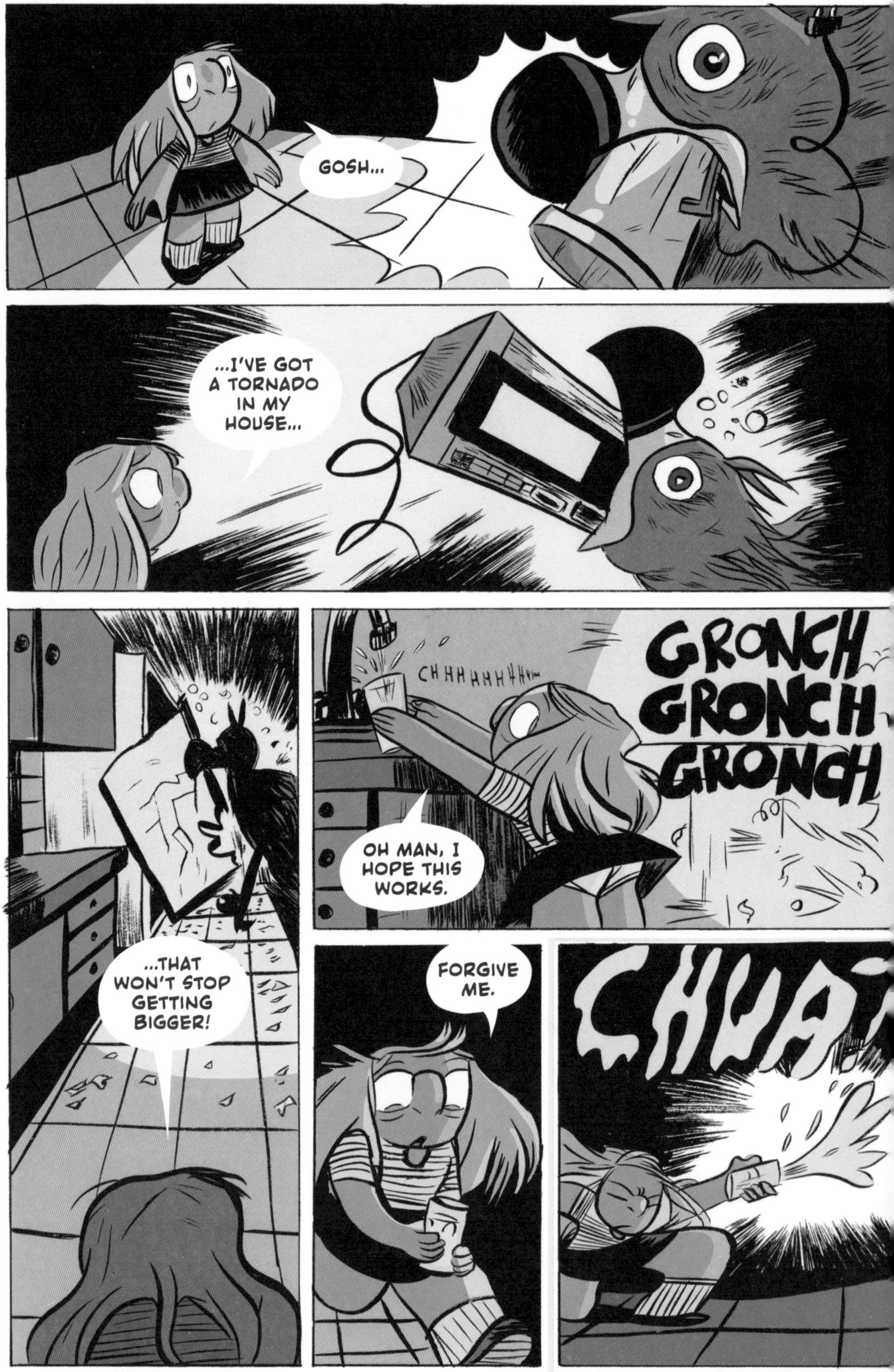
GOSH...
...I'VE GOT A TORNADO IN MY HOUSE...
...THAT WON'T STOP GETTING BIGGER!
CHHHHHHHH
GRONCH
GRONCH
GRONCH
OH MAN, I HOPE THIS WORKS.
FORGIVE ME.

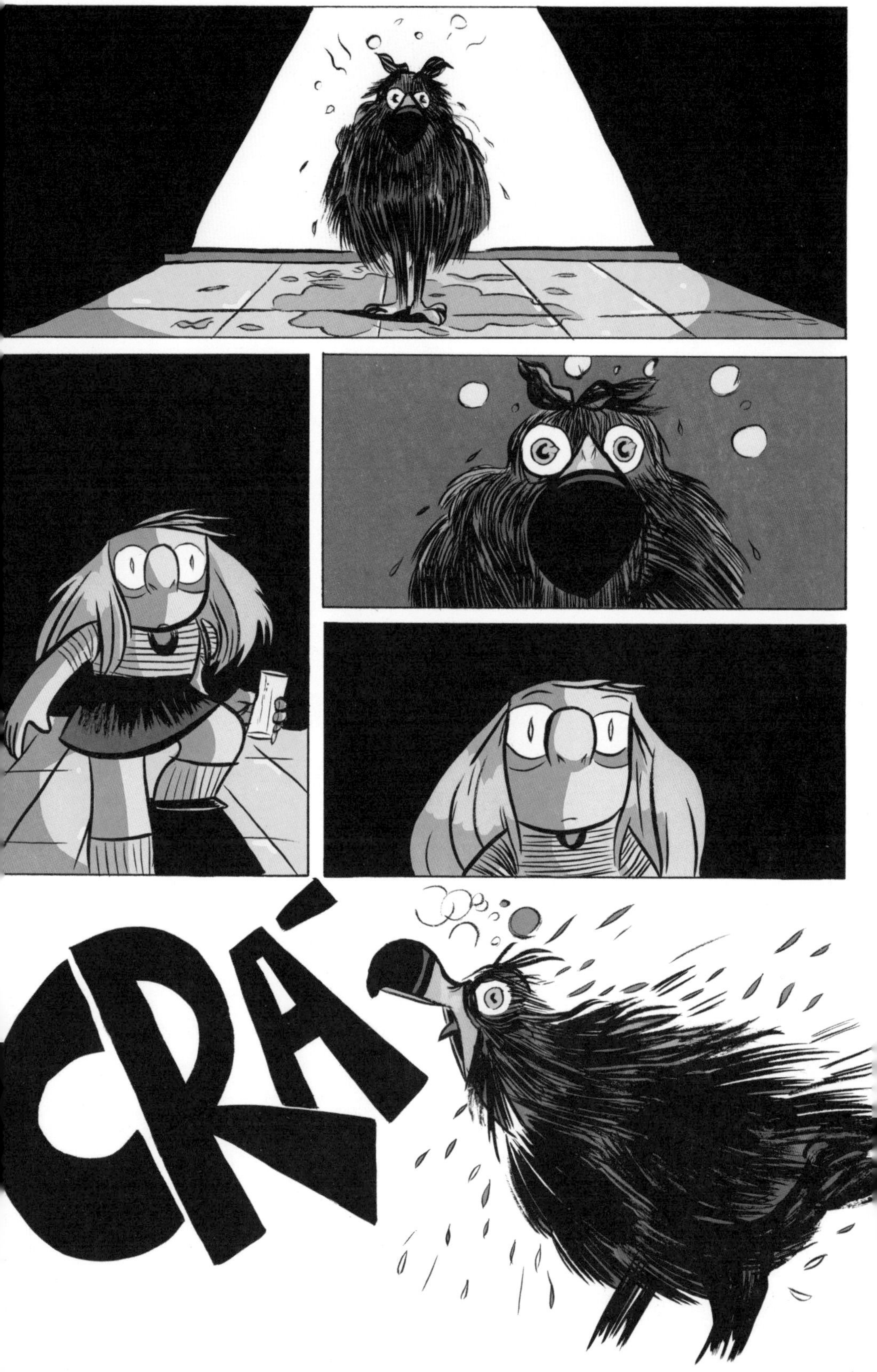
CRÁ

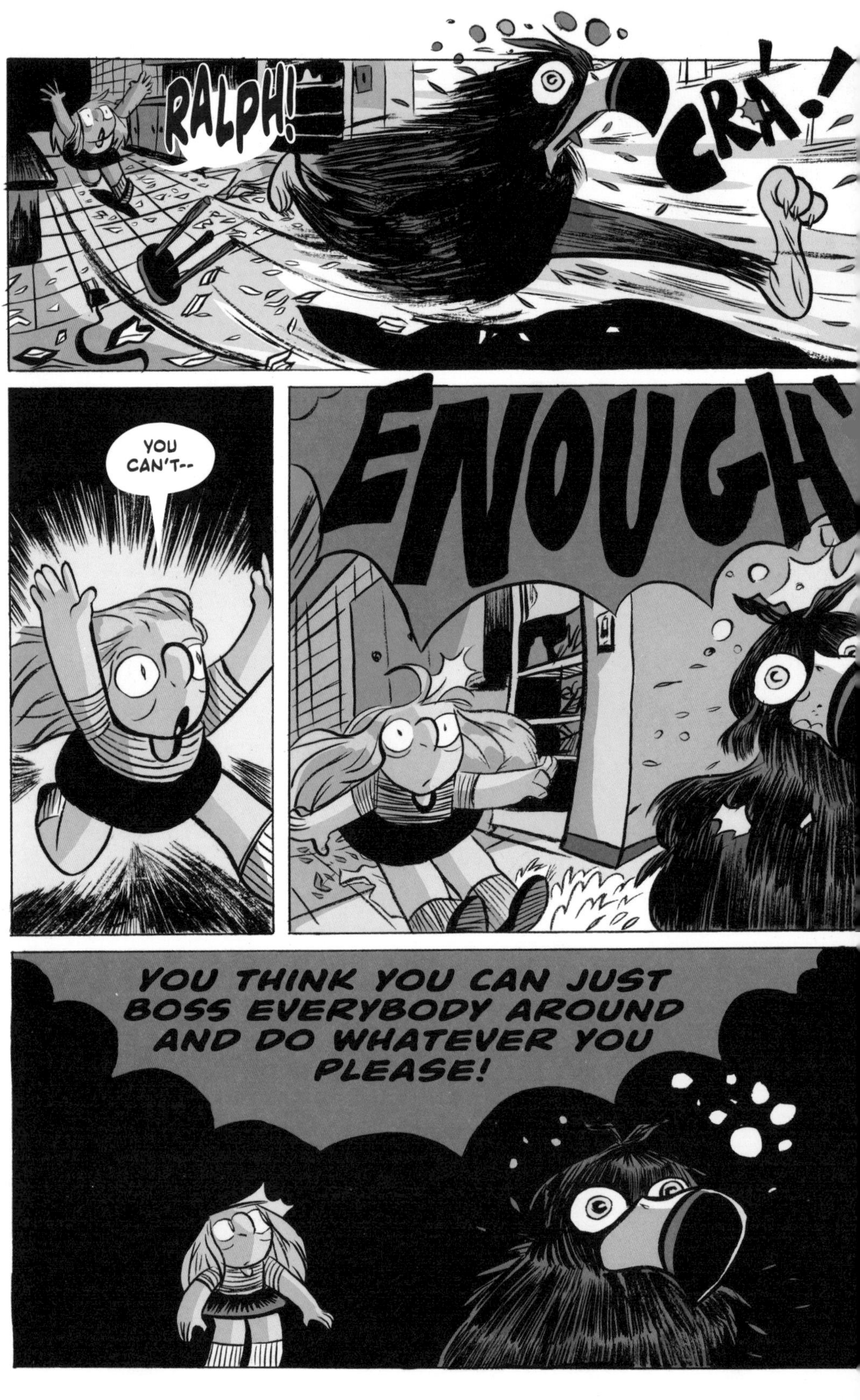
RALPH!
CRA!
YOU CAN'T--
ENOUGH
YOU THINK YOU CAN JUST BOSS EVERYBODY AROUND AND DO WHATEVER YOU PLEASE!

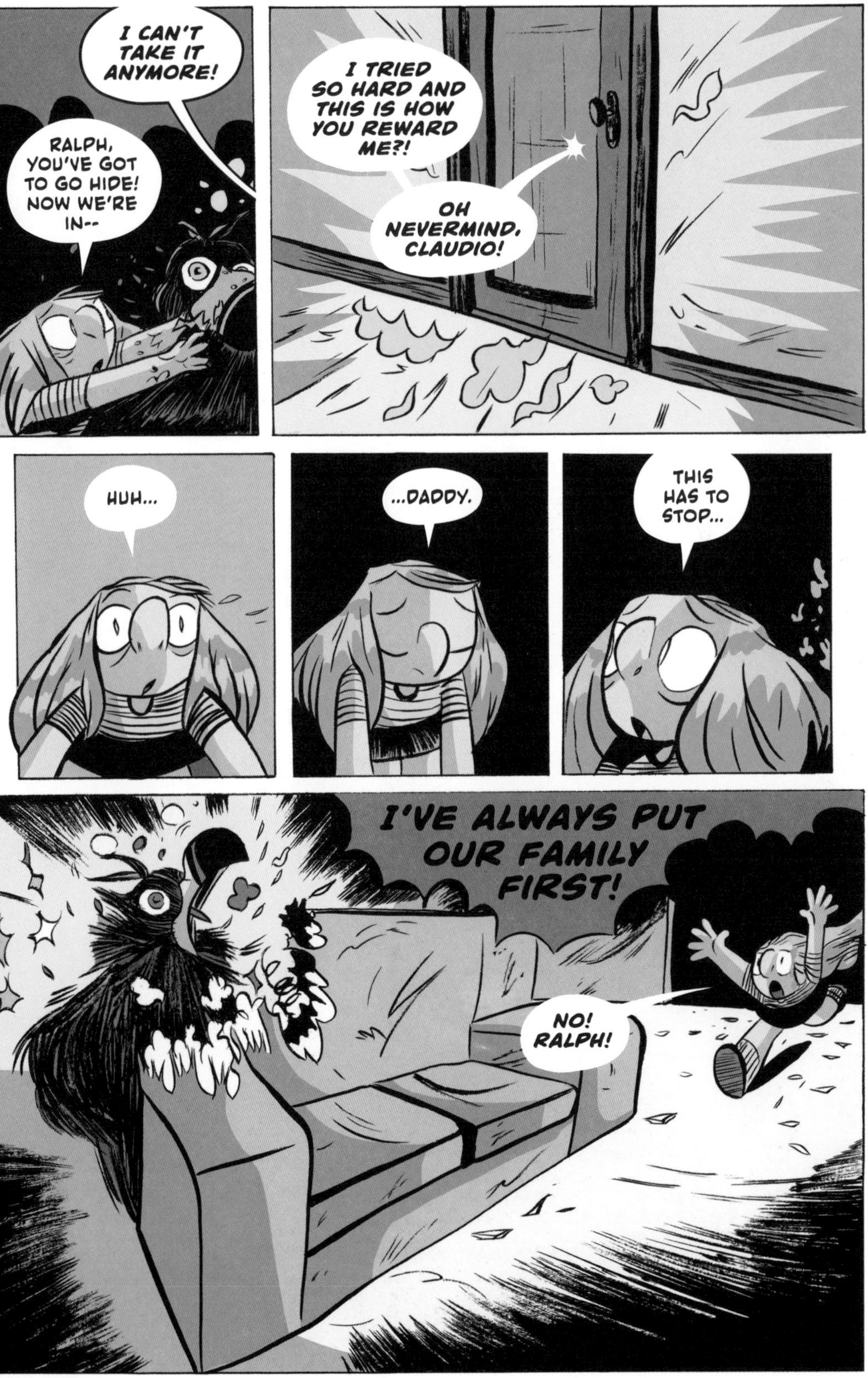
I CAN'T TAKE IT ANYMORE!
RALPH, YOU'VE GOT TO GO HIDE! NOW WE'RE IN--
I TRIED SO HARD AND THIS IS HOW YOU REWARD ME?!
OH NEVERMIND, CLAUDIO!
HUH...
...DADDY.
THIS HAS TO STOP...
I'VE ALWAYS PUT OUR FAMILY FIRST!
NO! RALPH!

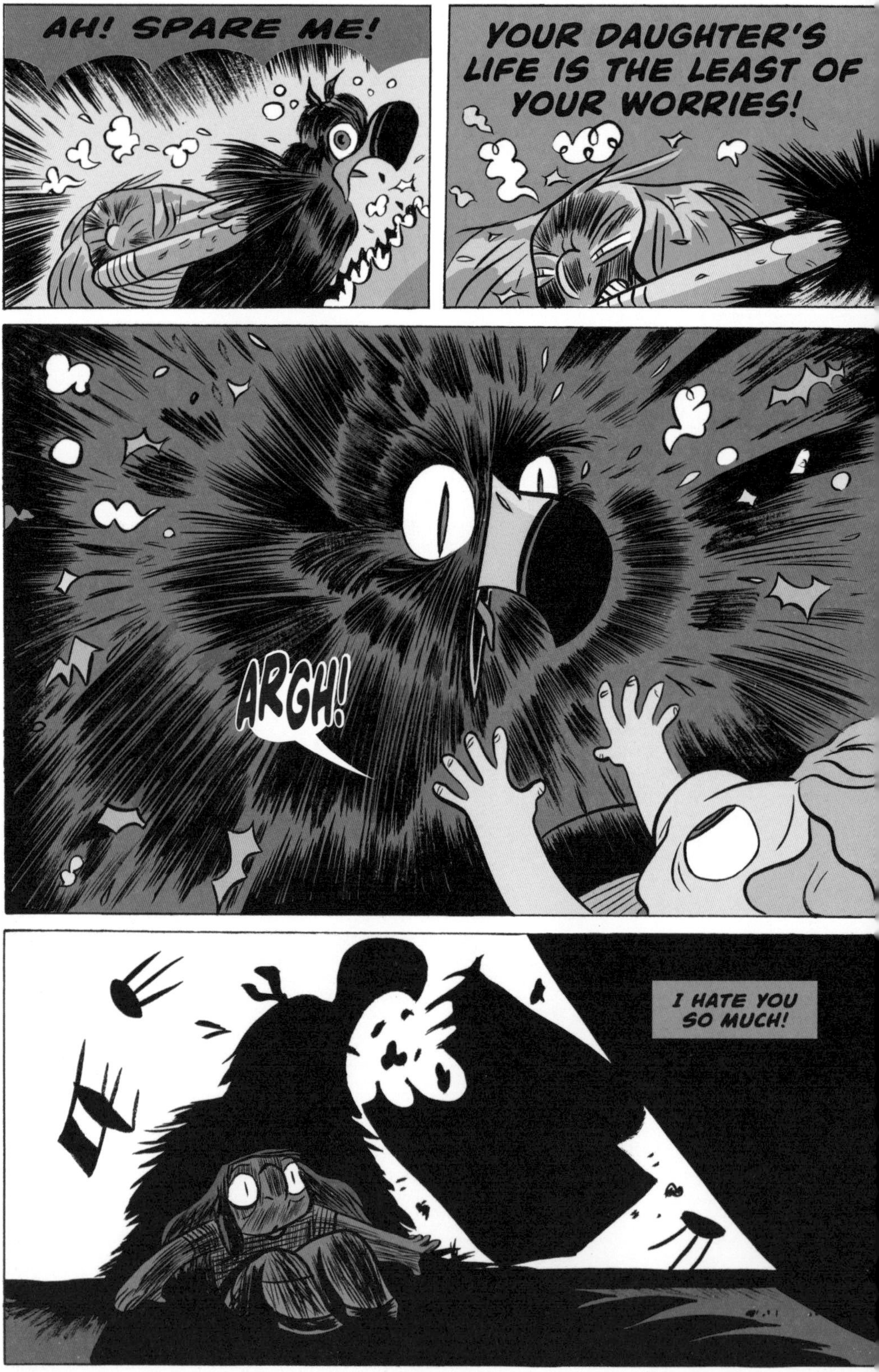
AH! SPARE ME!
YOUR DAUGHTER'S LIFE IS THE LEAST OF YOUR WORRIES!
ARGH!
I HATE YOU SO MUCH!

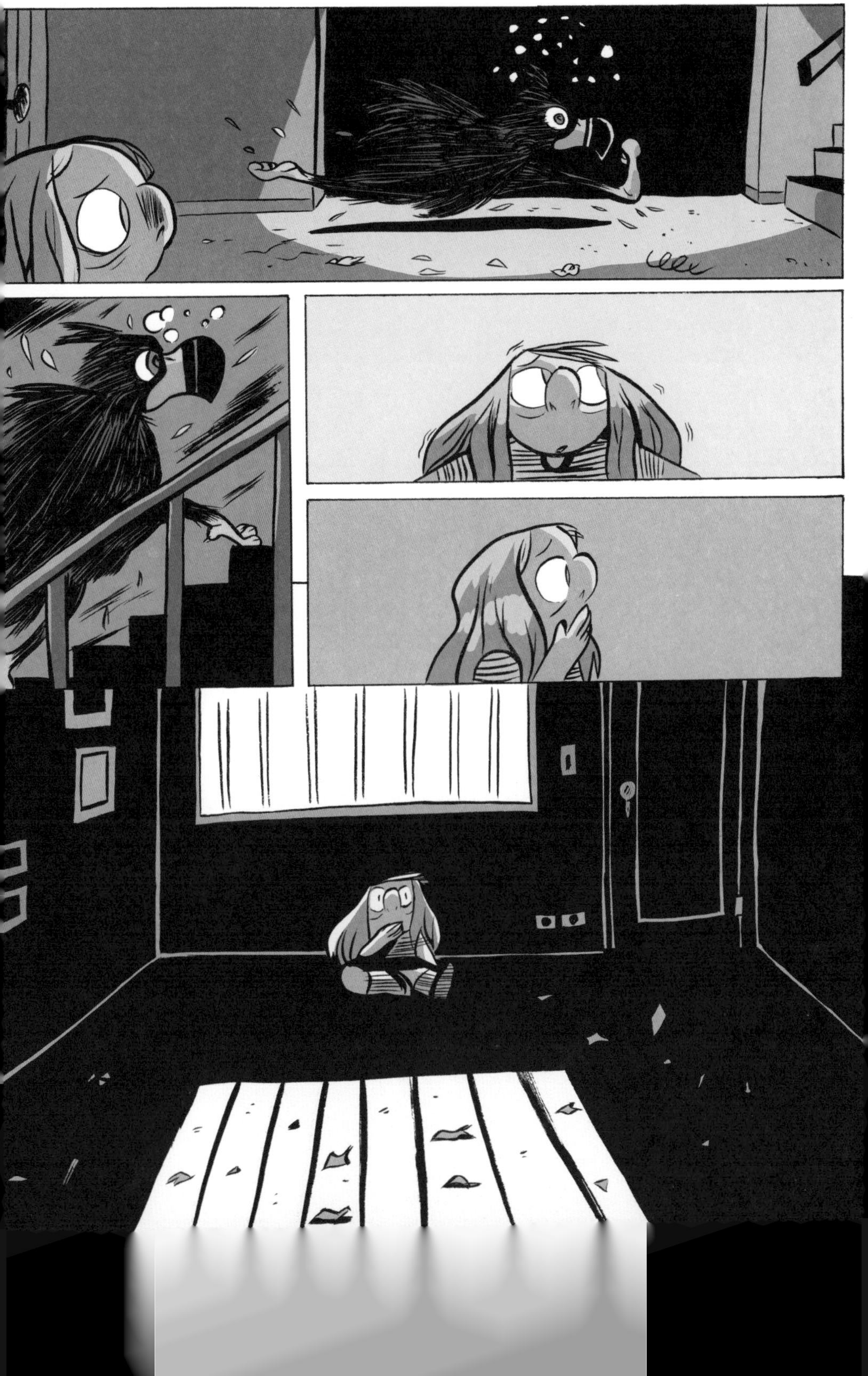

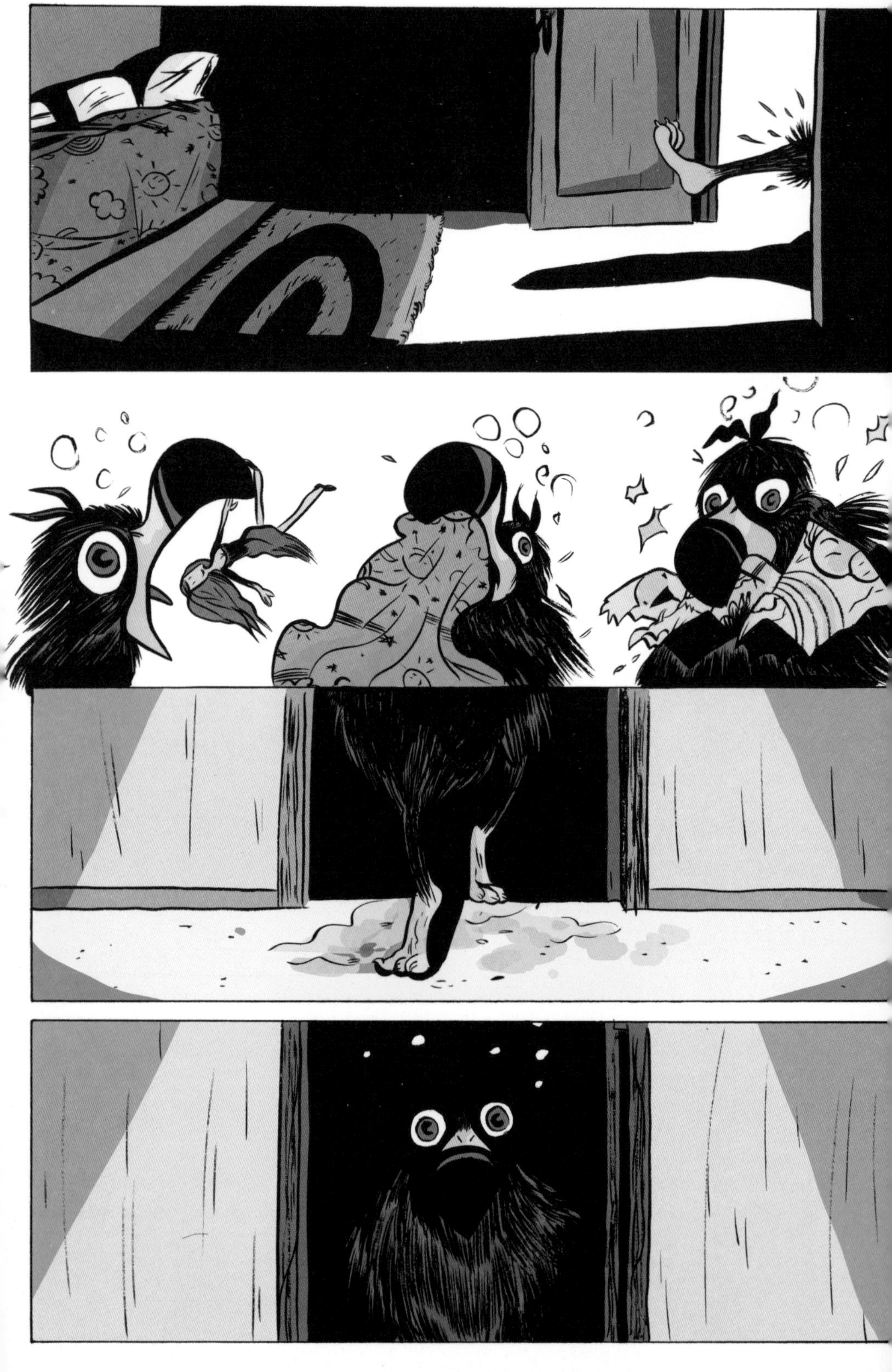

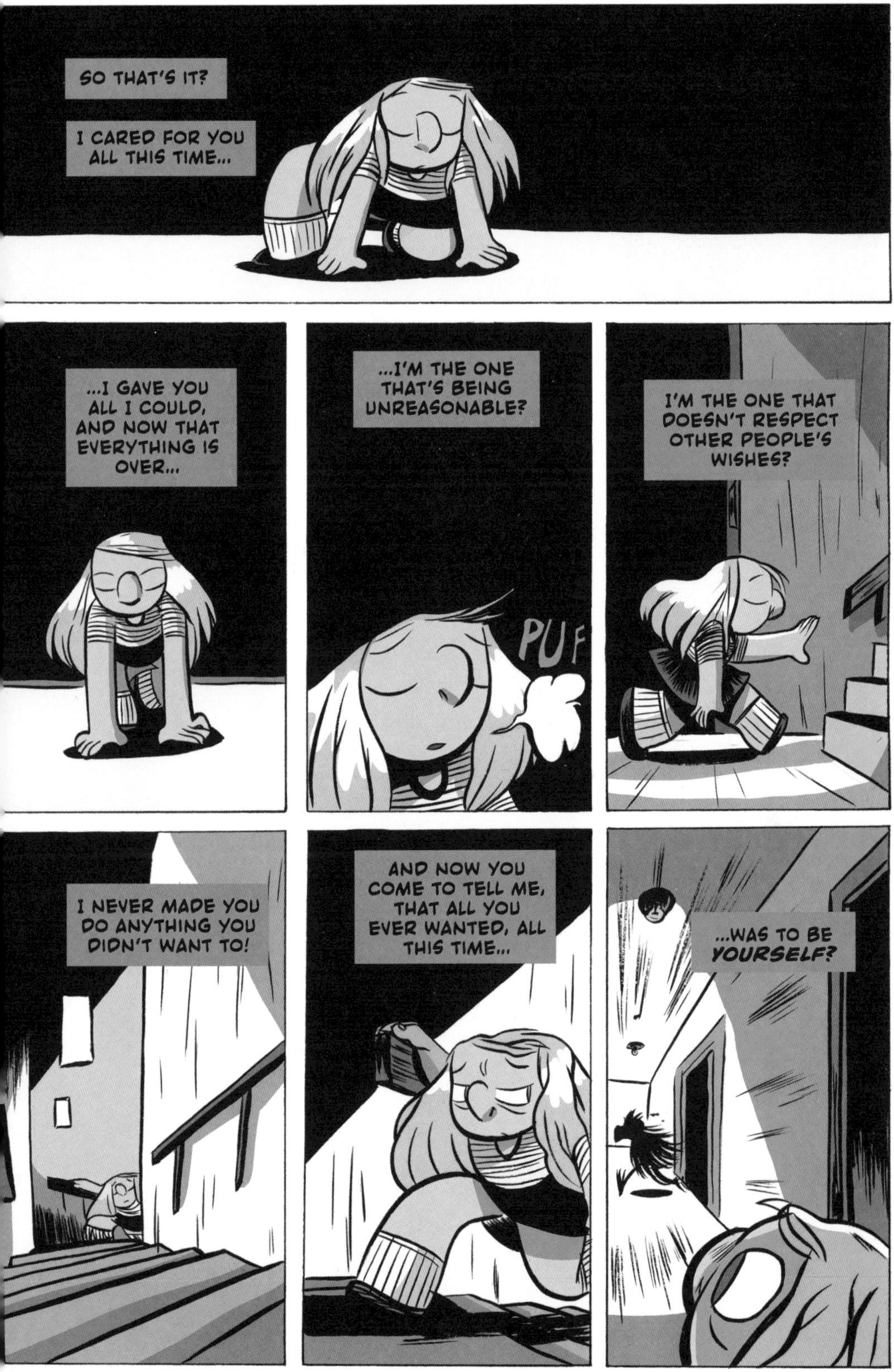
SO THAT'S IT?
I CARED FOR YOU ALL THIS TIME...
...I GAVE YOU ALL I COULD, AND NOW THAT EVERYTHING IS OVER...
...I'M THE ONE THAT'S BEING UNREASONABLE?
PUF
I'M THE ONE THAT DOESN'T RESPECT OTHER PEOPLE'S WISHES?
I NEVER MADE YOU DO ANYTHING YOU DIDN'T WANT TO!
AND NOW YOU COME TO TELL ME, THAT ALL YOU EVER WANTED, ALL THIS TIME...
...WAS TO BE *YOURSELF?*

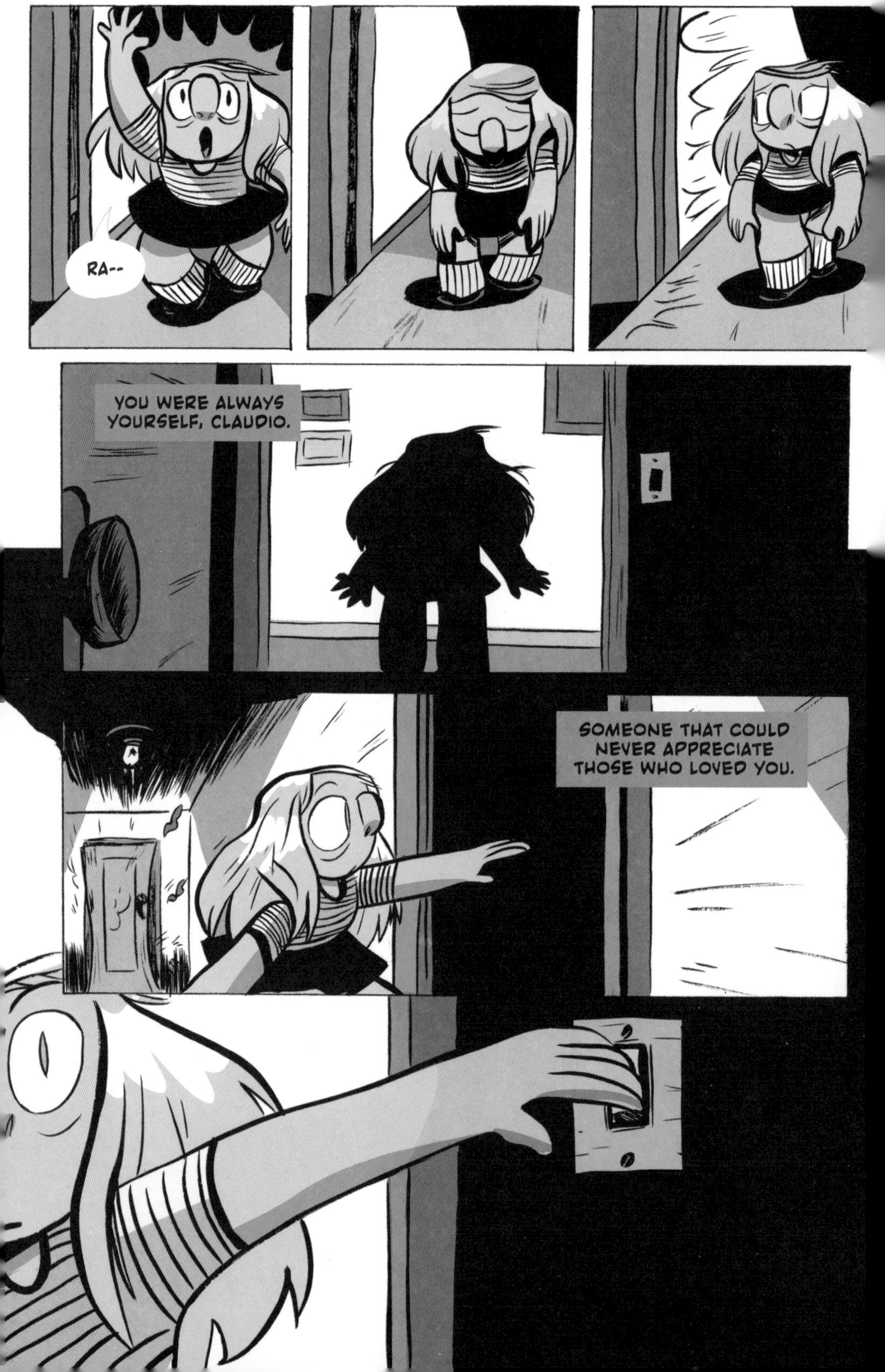
RA--
YOU WERE ALWAYS YOURSELF, CLAUDIO.
SOMEONE THAT COULD NEVER APPRECIATE THOSE WHO LOVED YOU.

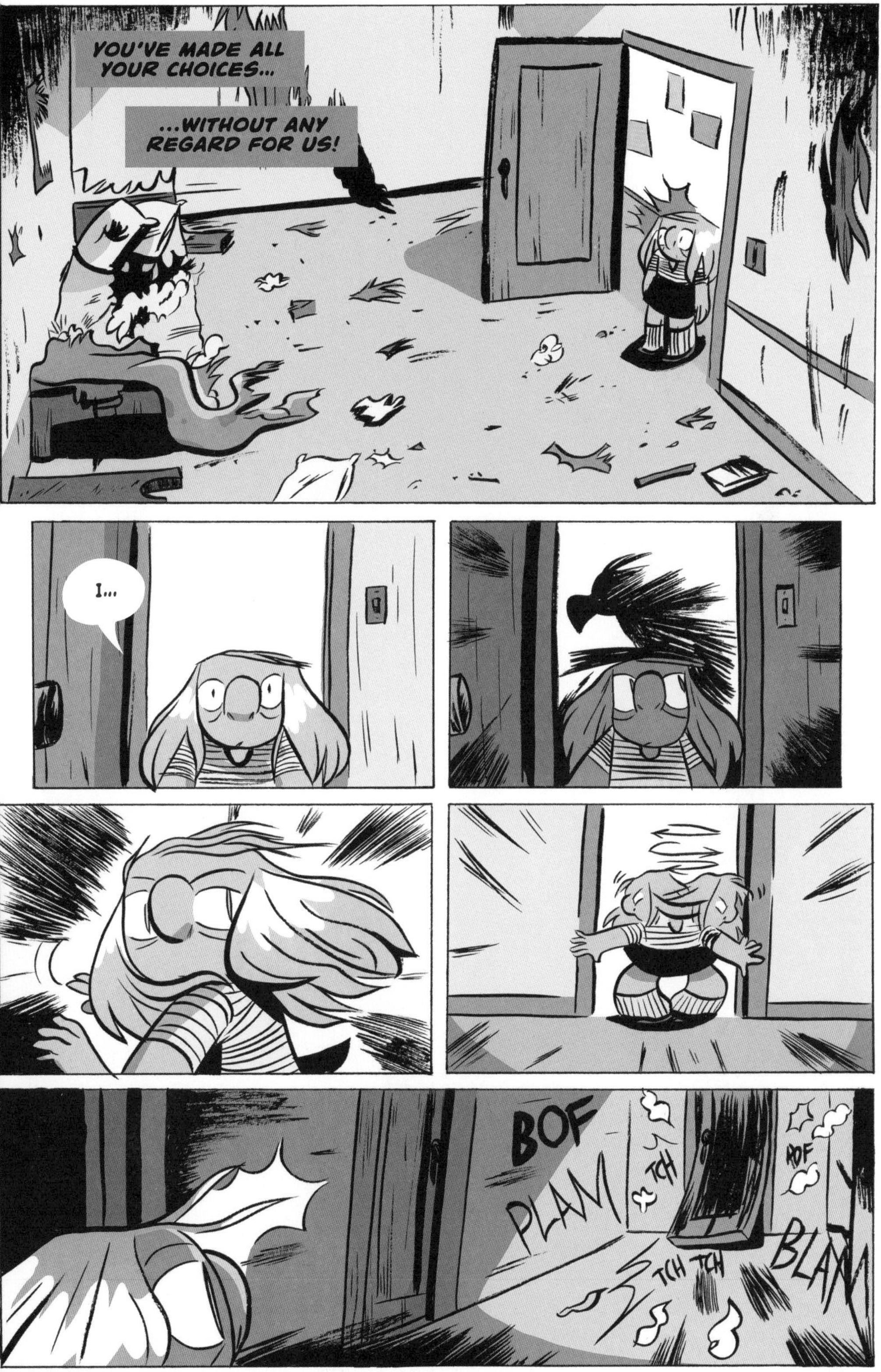
YOU'VE MADE ALL YOUR CHOICES...
...WITHOUT ANY REGARD FOR US!
I...
BOF
PLAM
TCH
ROF
TCH TCH
BLAM

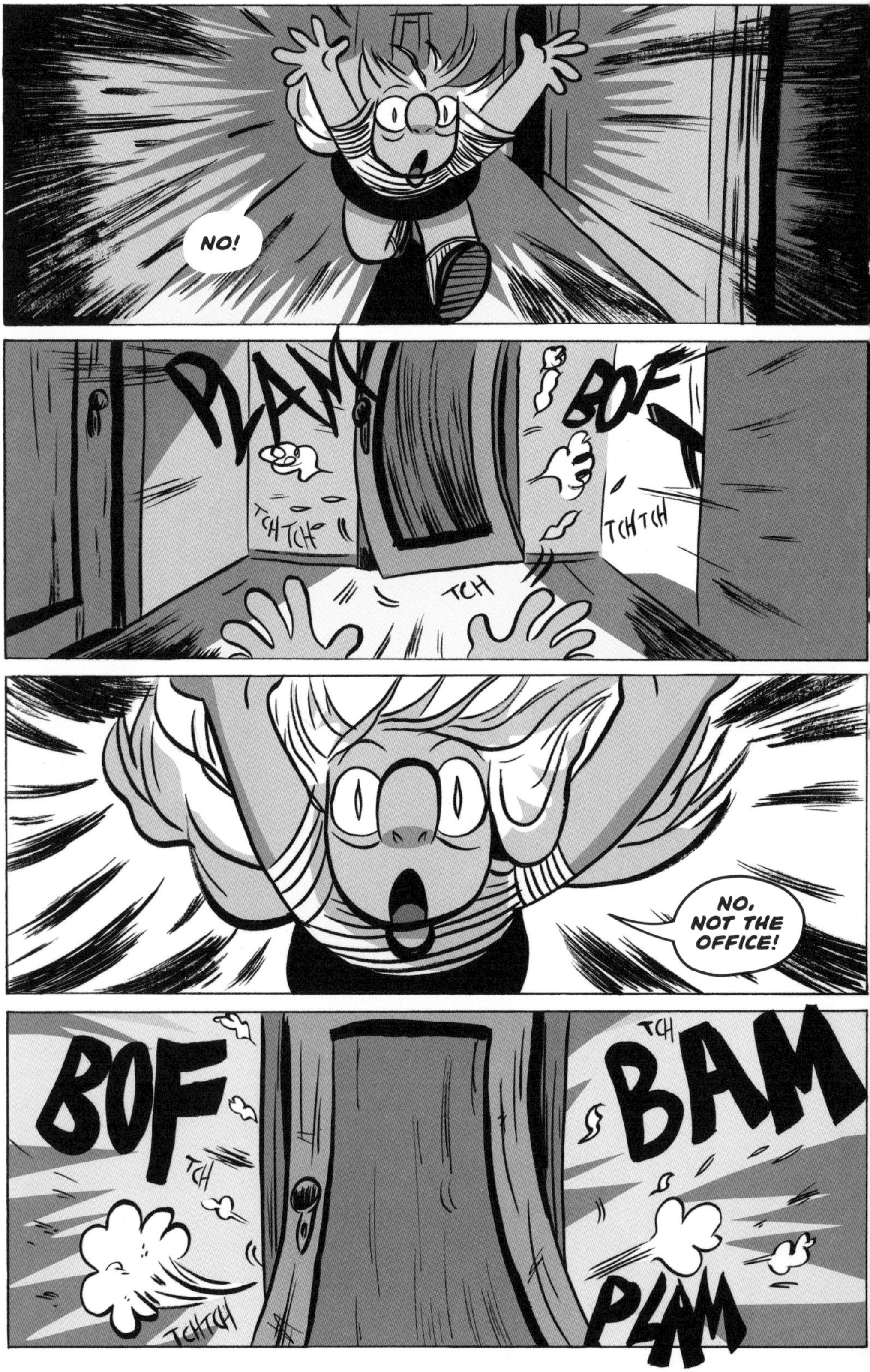
NO!
PLAM
BOF
TCHTCH
TCHTCH
TCH
NO, NOT THE OFFICE!
BOF
TCH
TCHTCH
TCH
BAM
PLAM

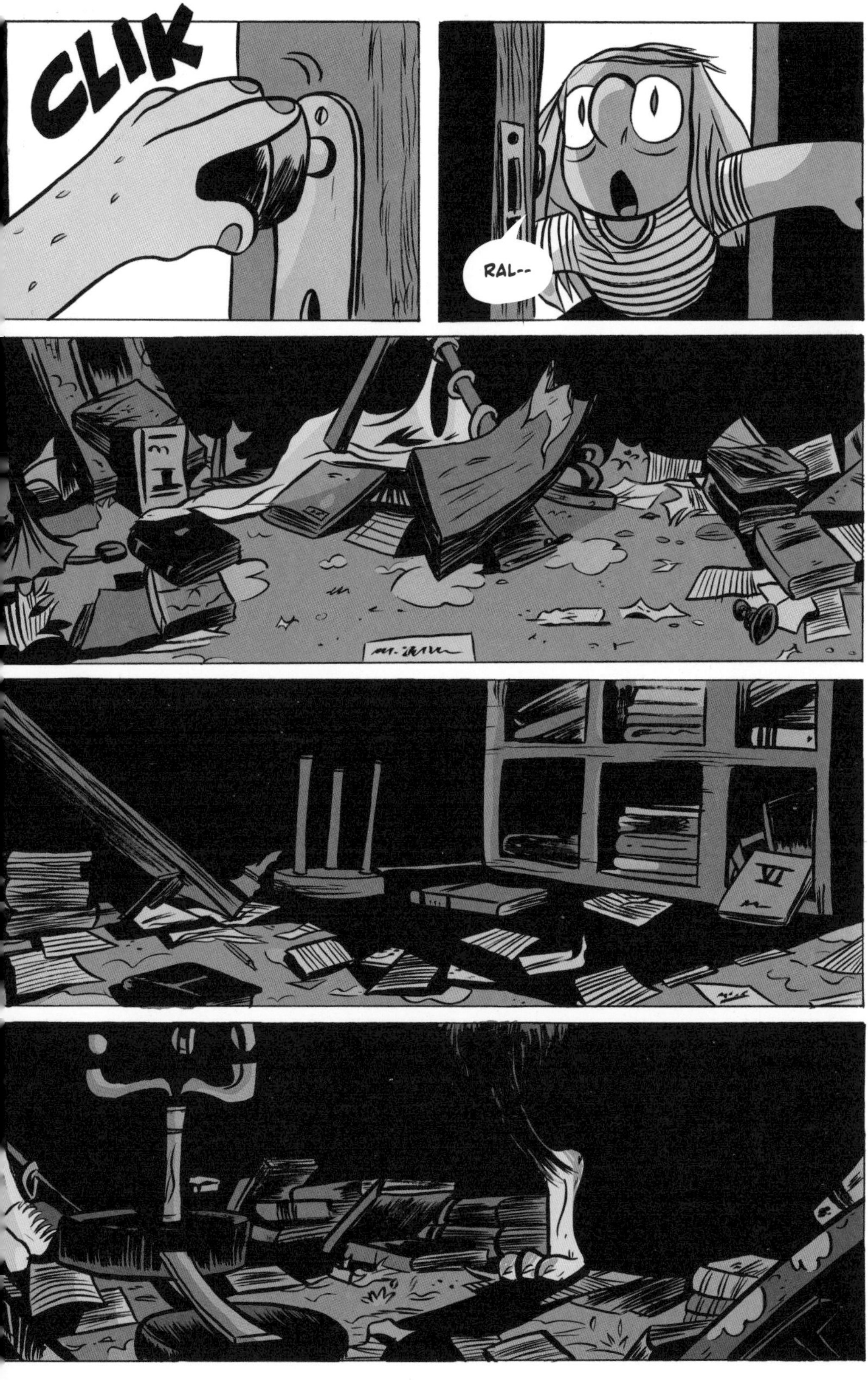
CLIK
RAL--

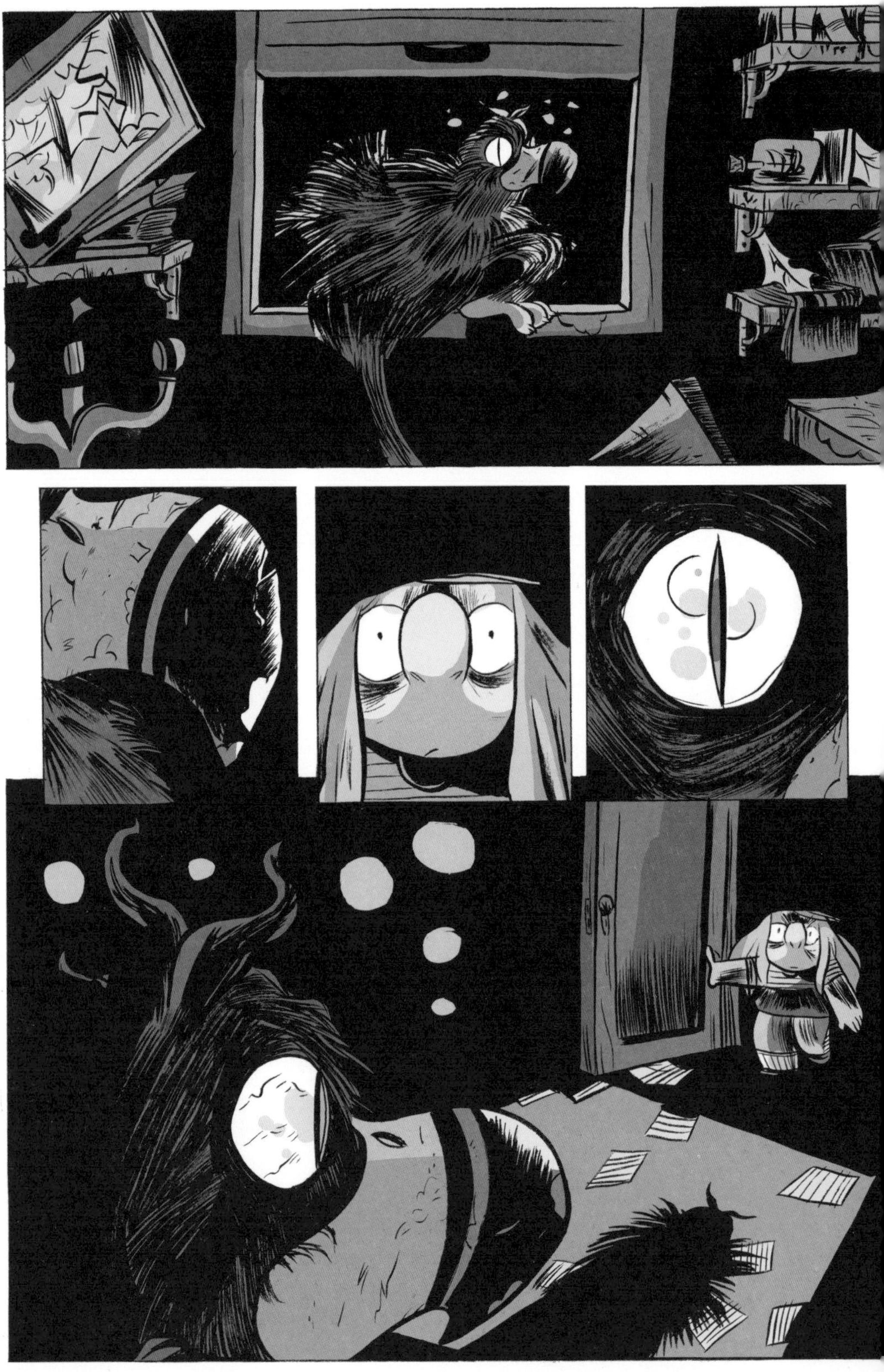

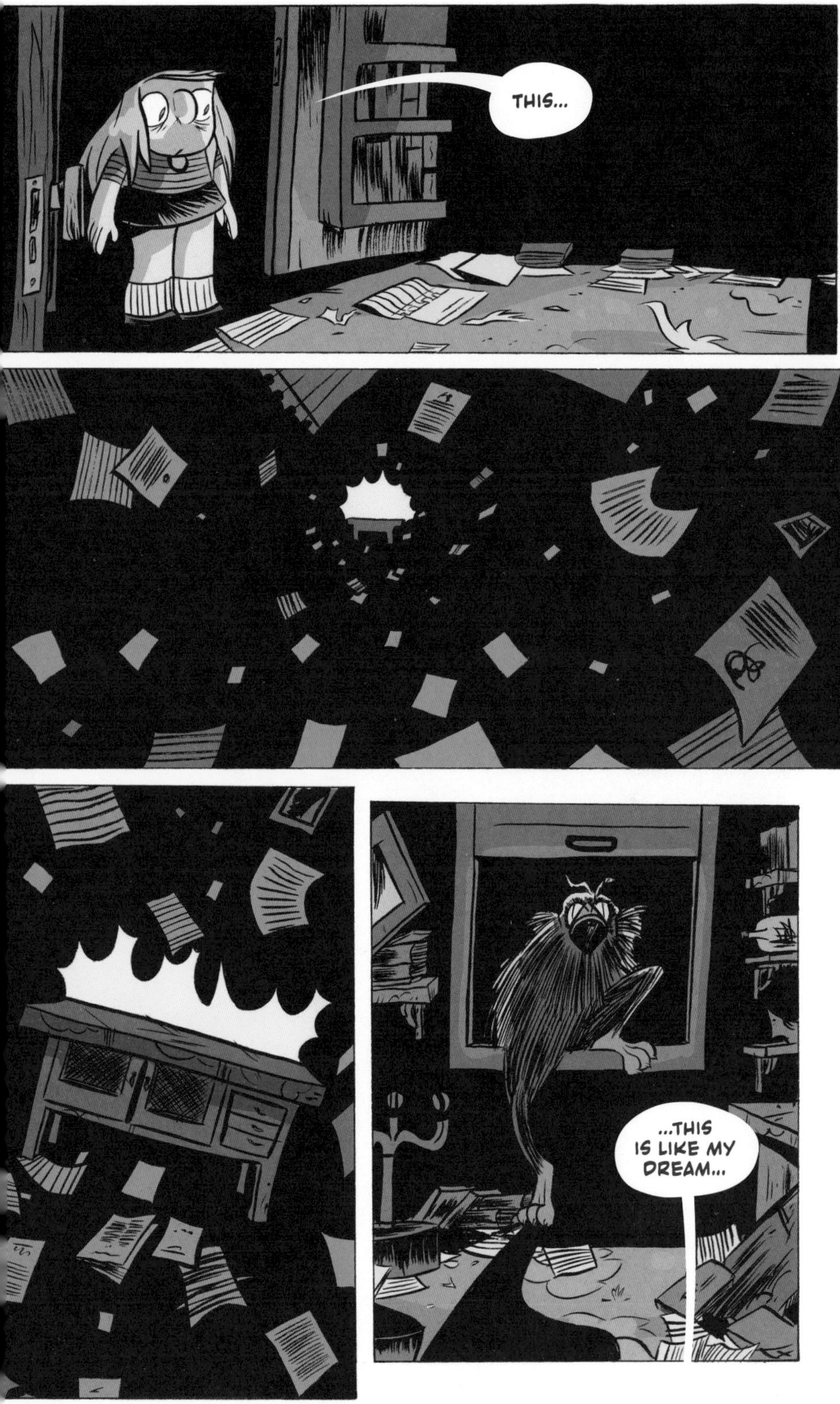
THIS...
...THIS IS LIKE MY DREAM...

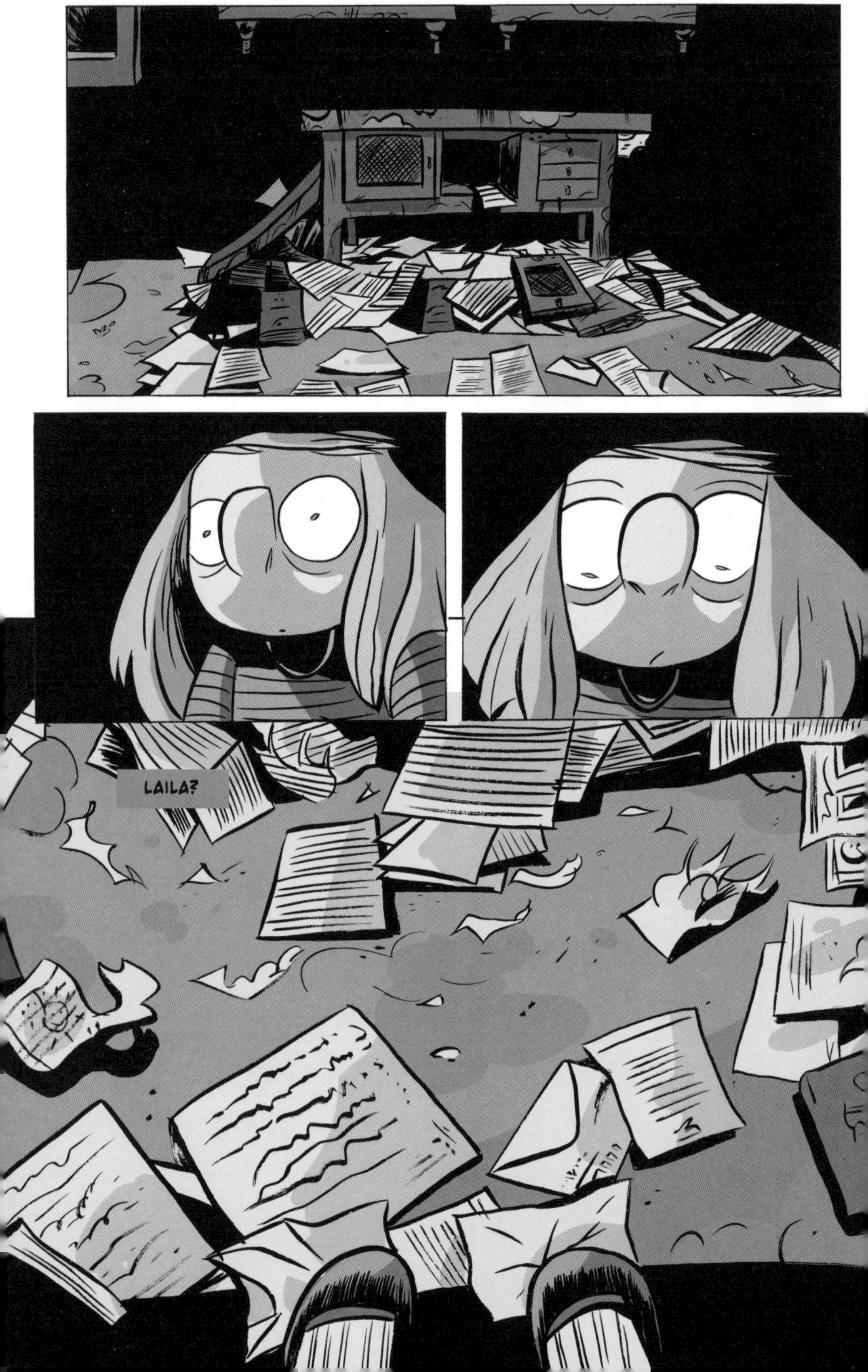
LAILA?

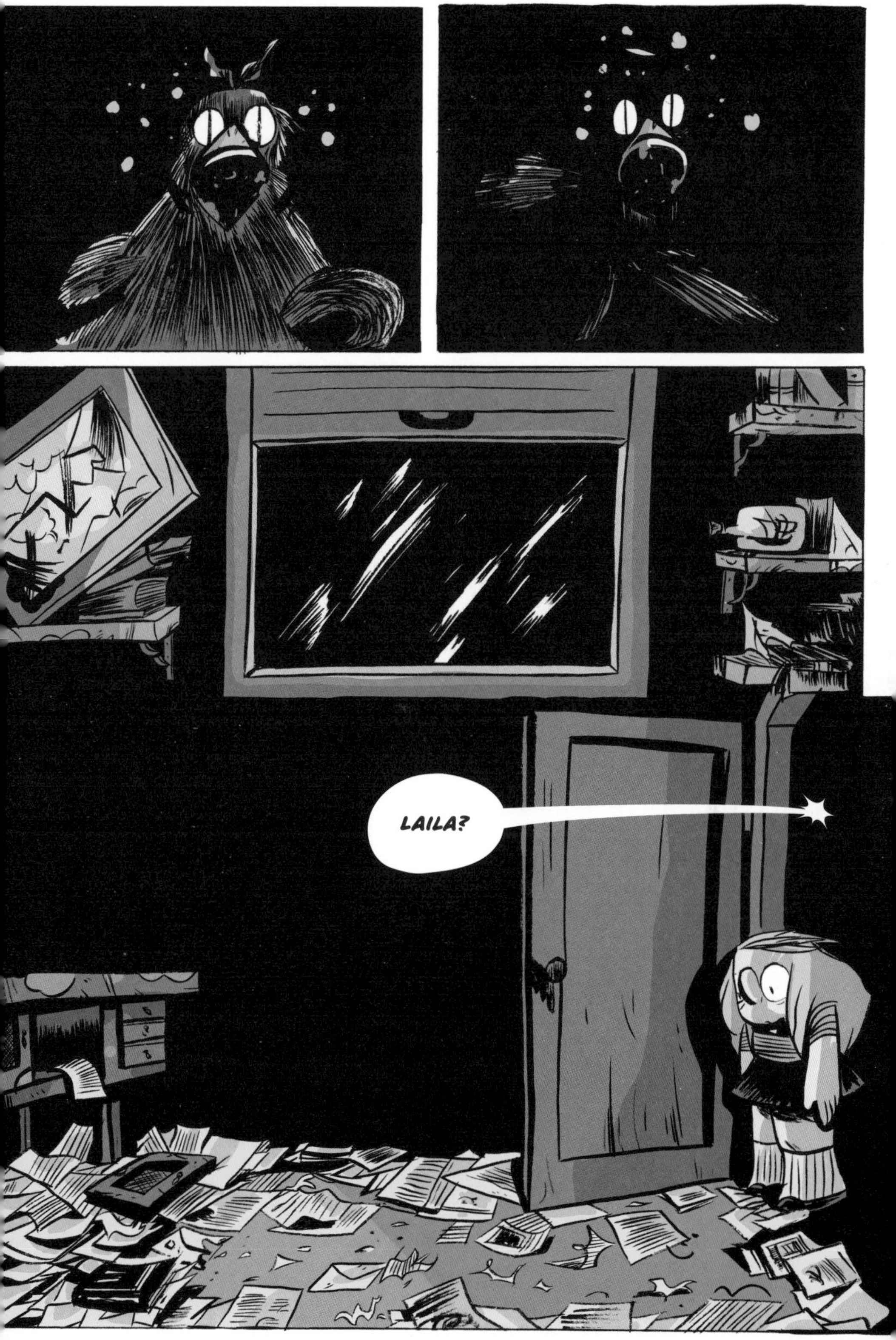
LAILA?

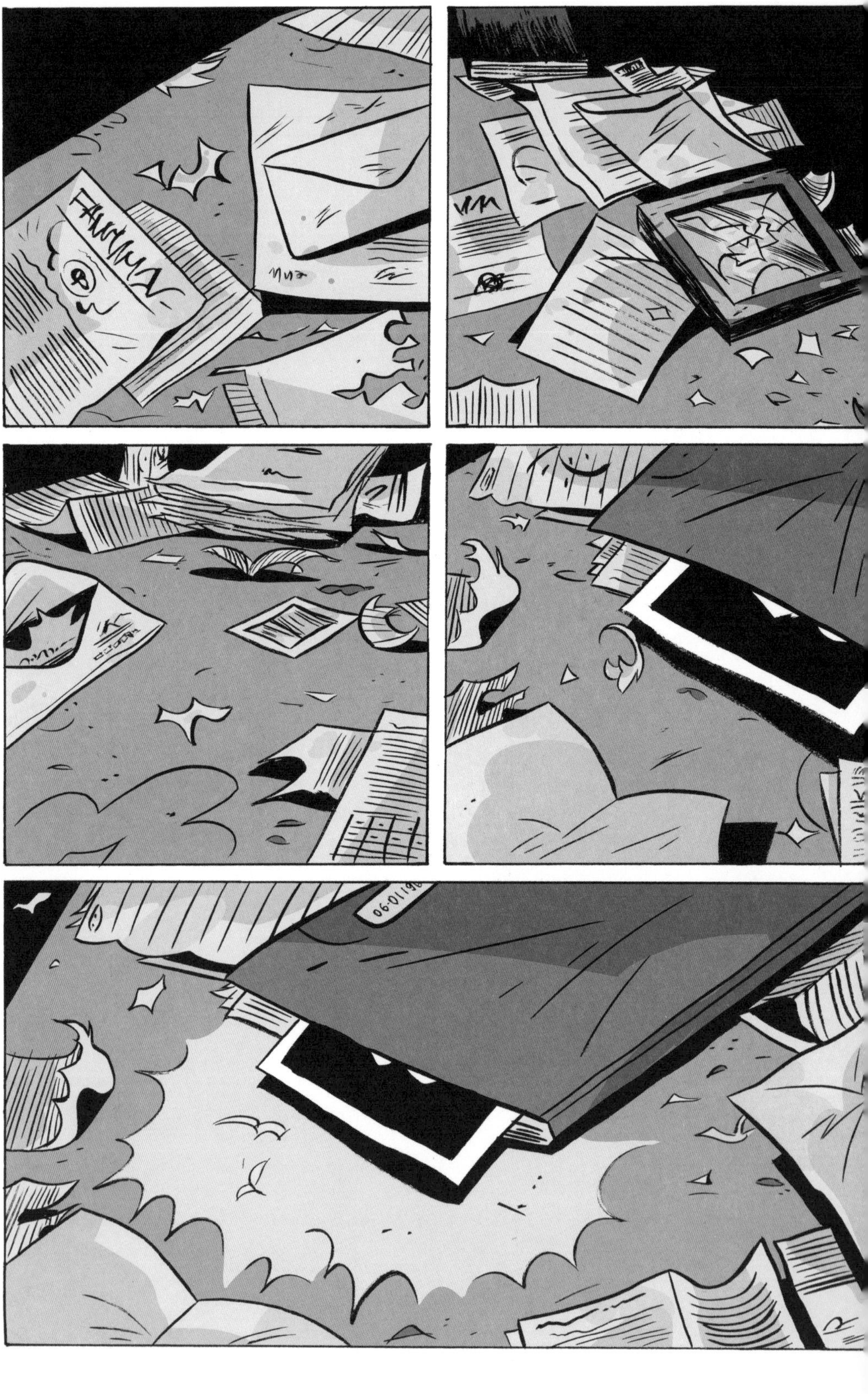

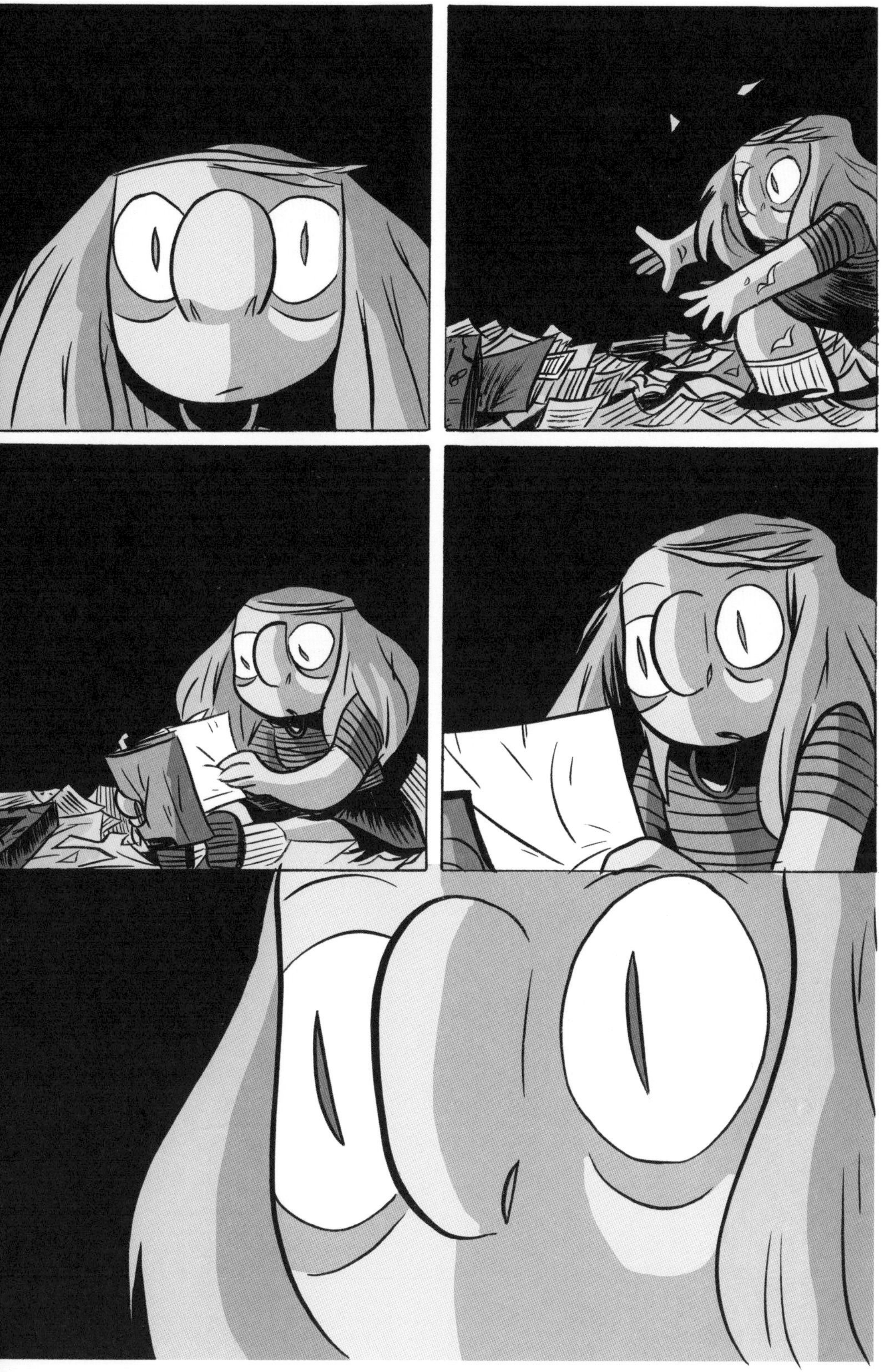

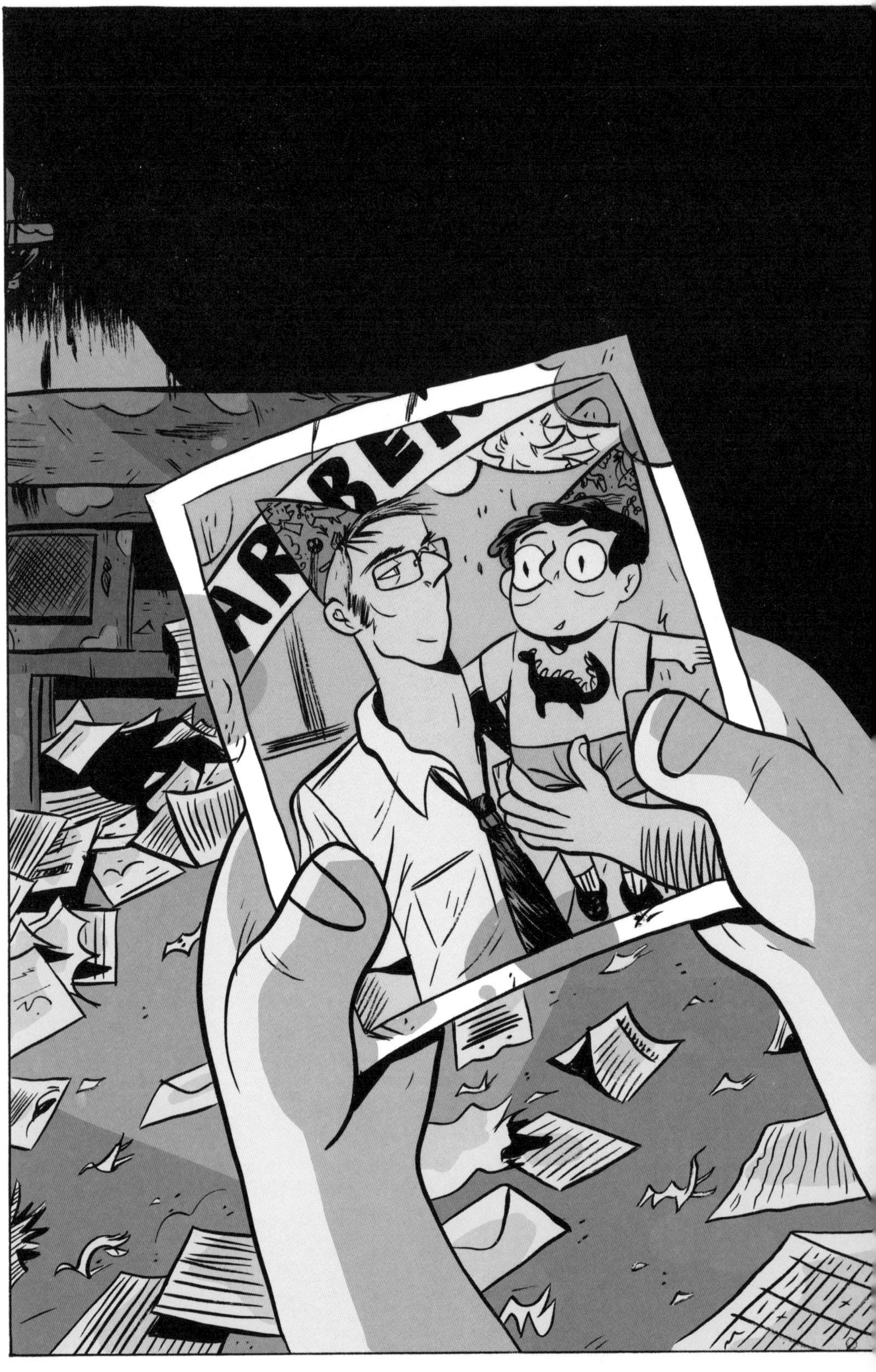

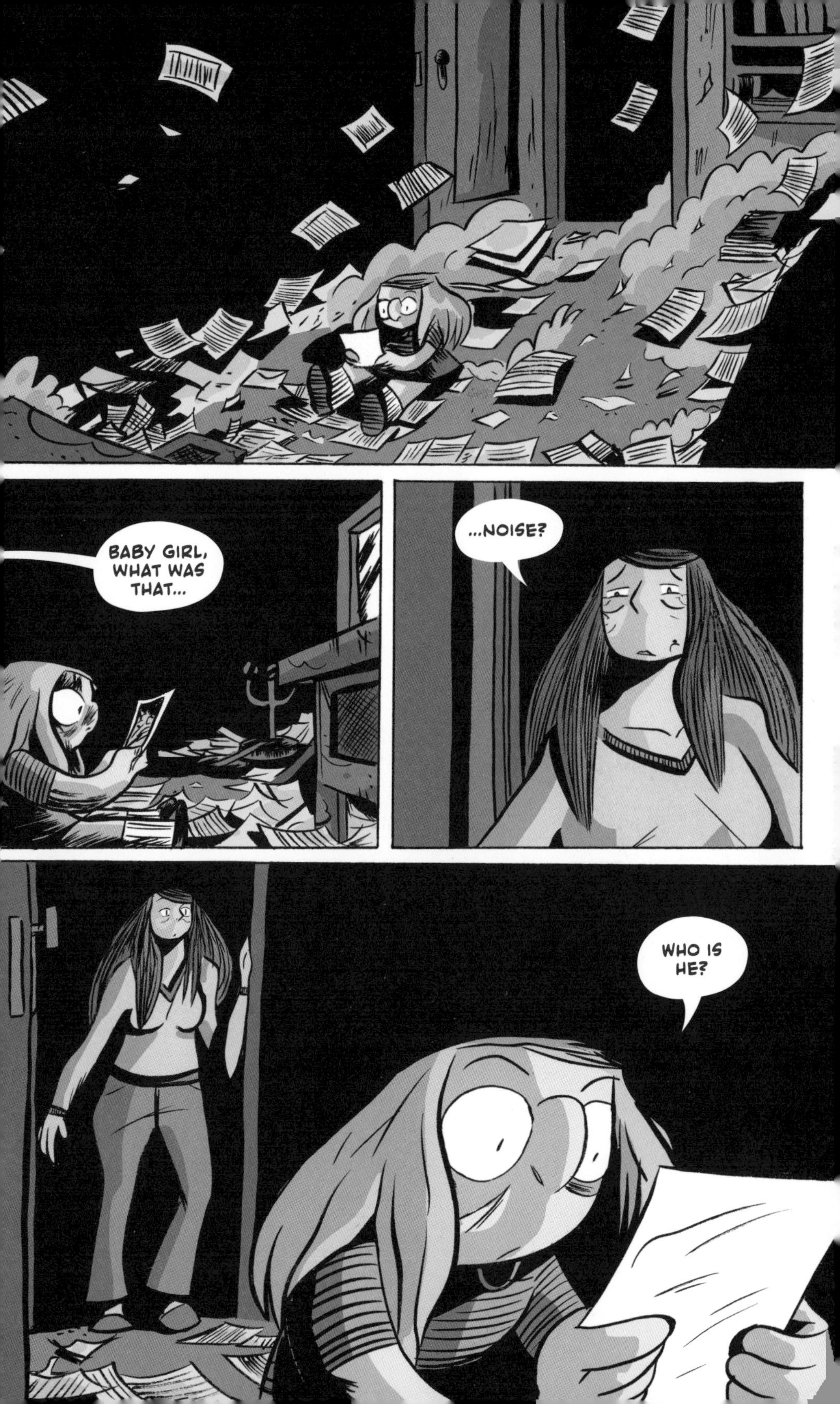
BABY GIRL, WHAT WAS THAT...
...NOISE?
WHO IS HE?

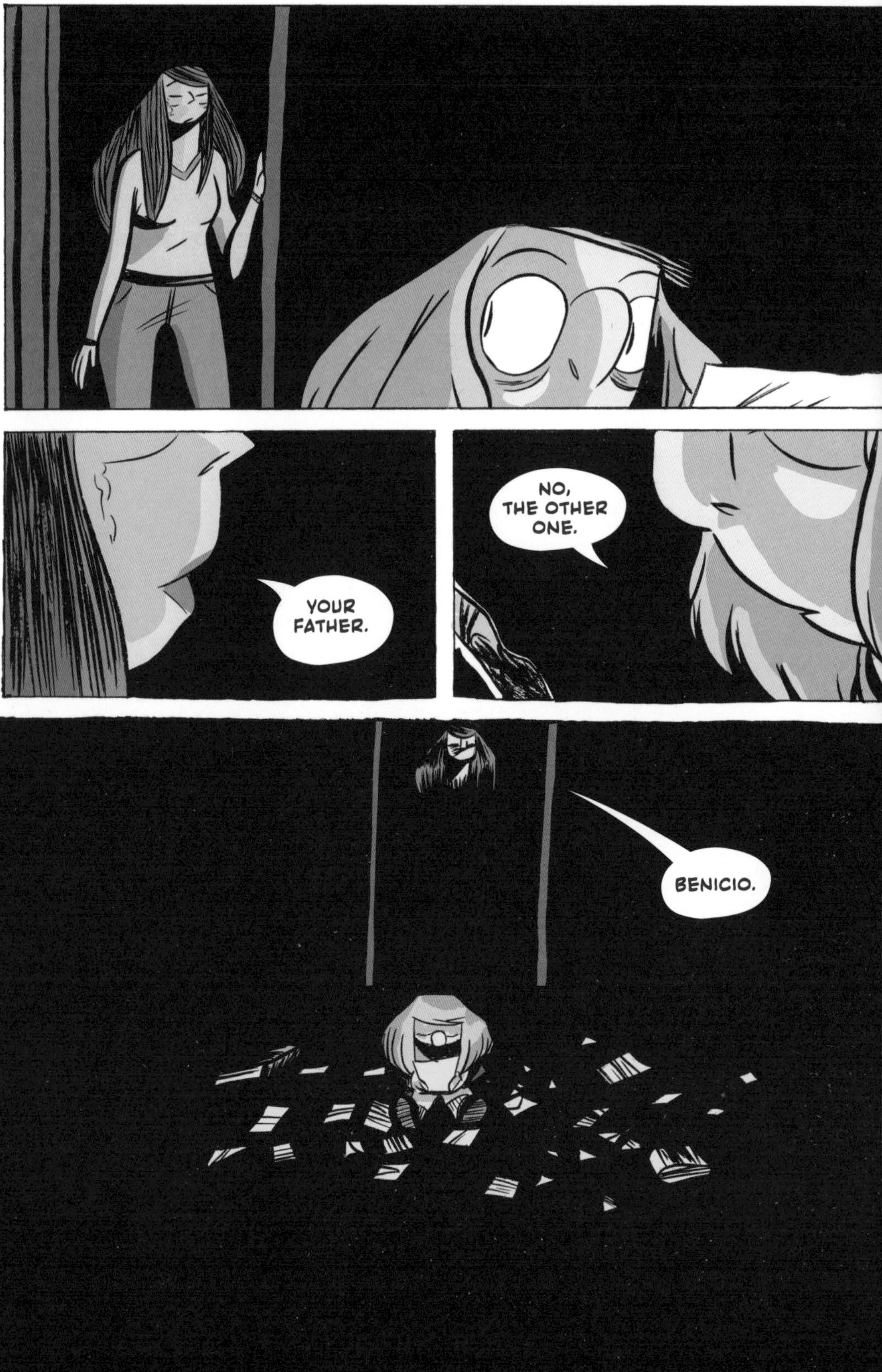
YOUR FATHER.
NO, THE OTHER ONE.
BENICIO.

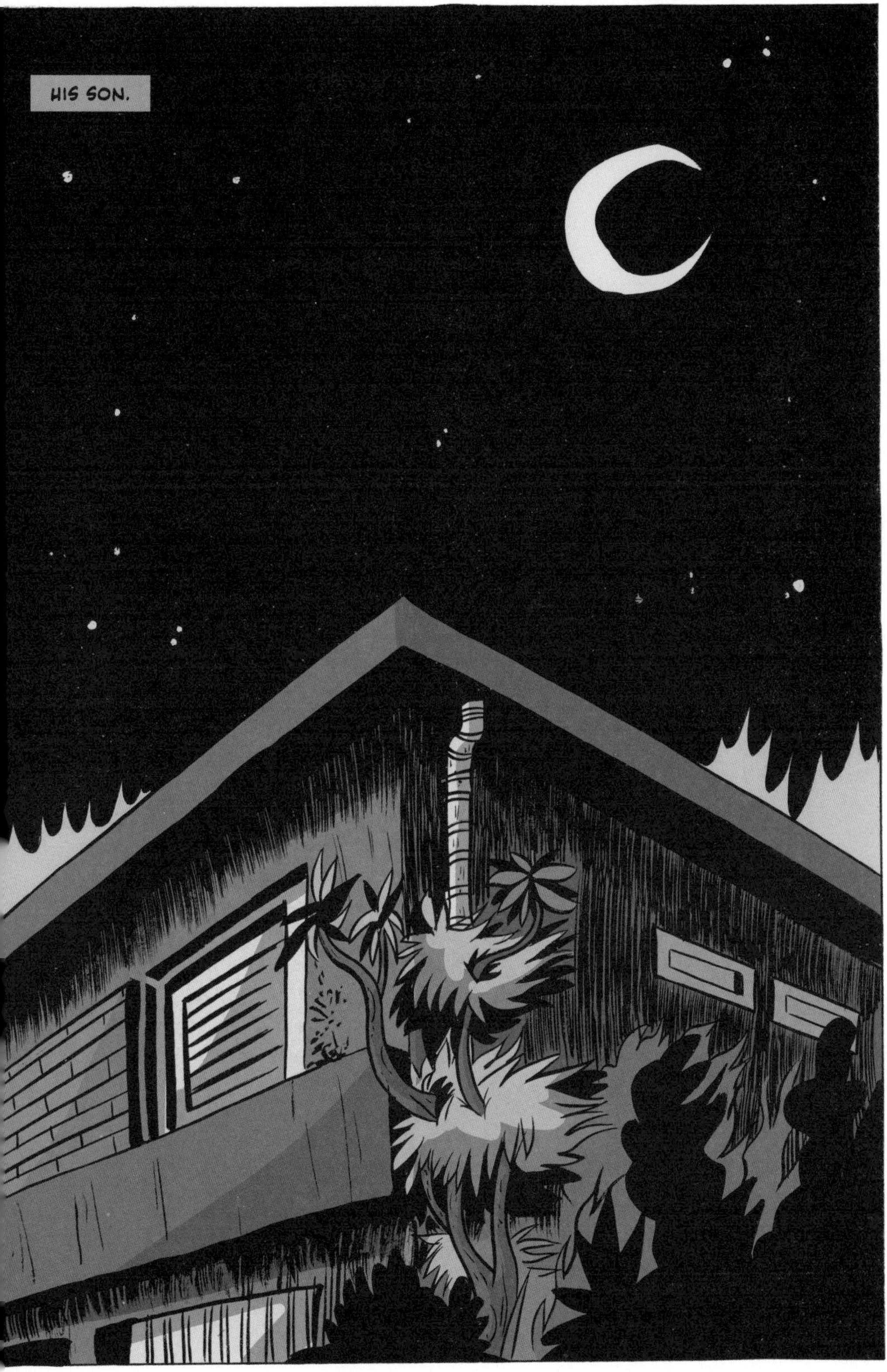
HIS SON.

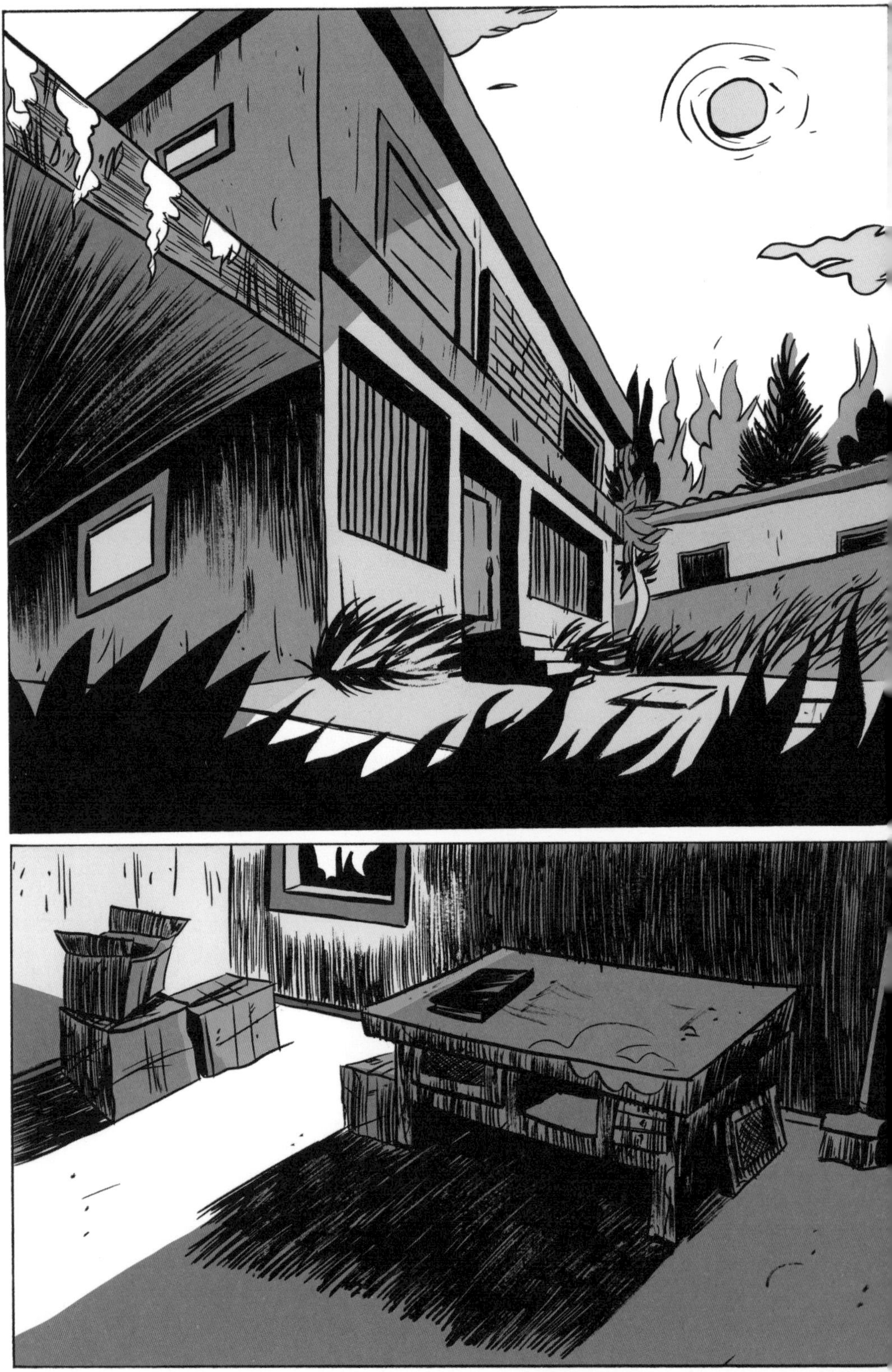

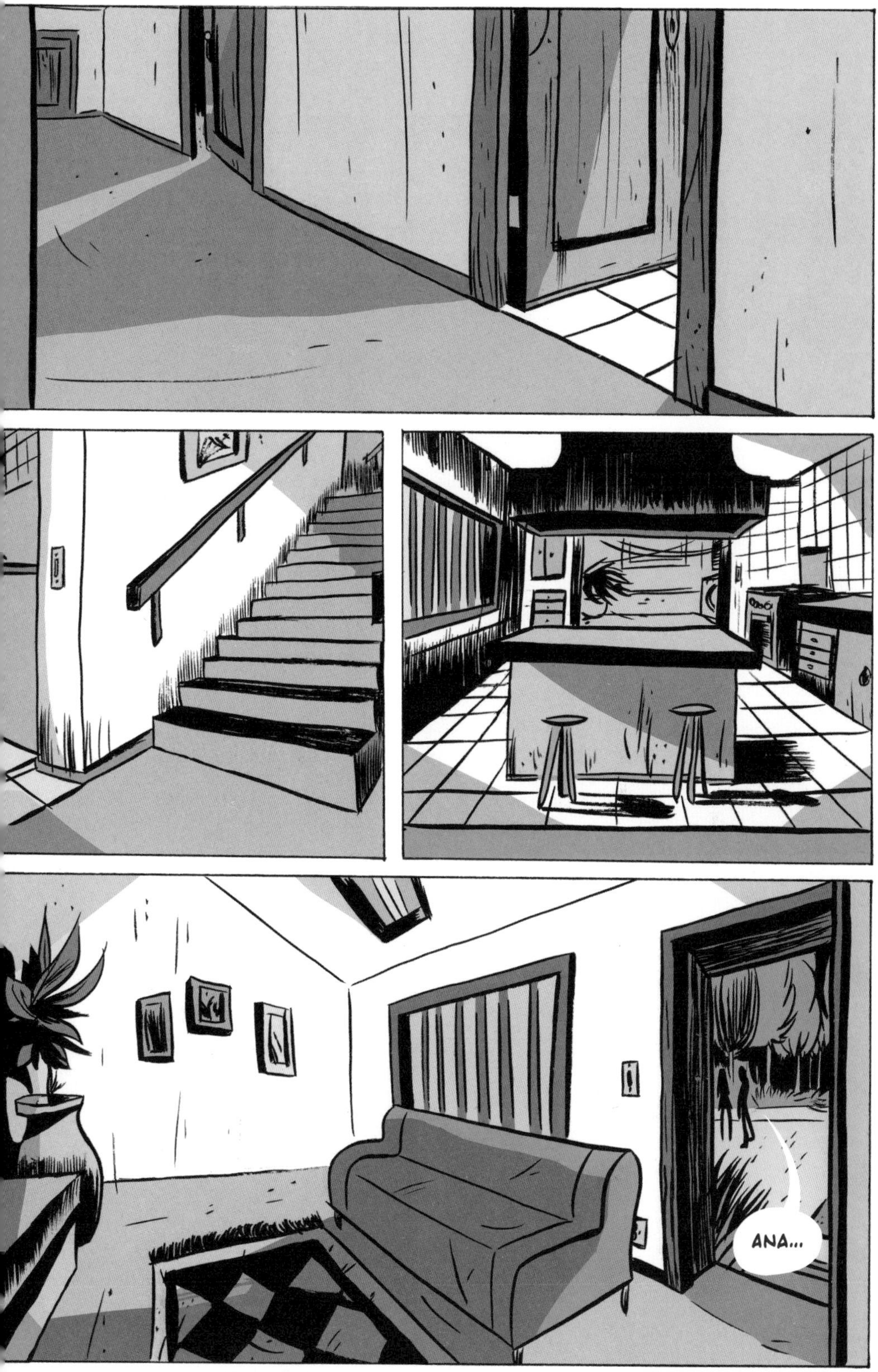
ANA...

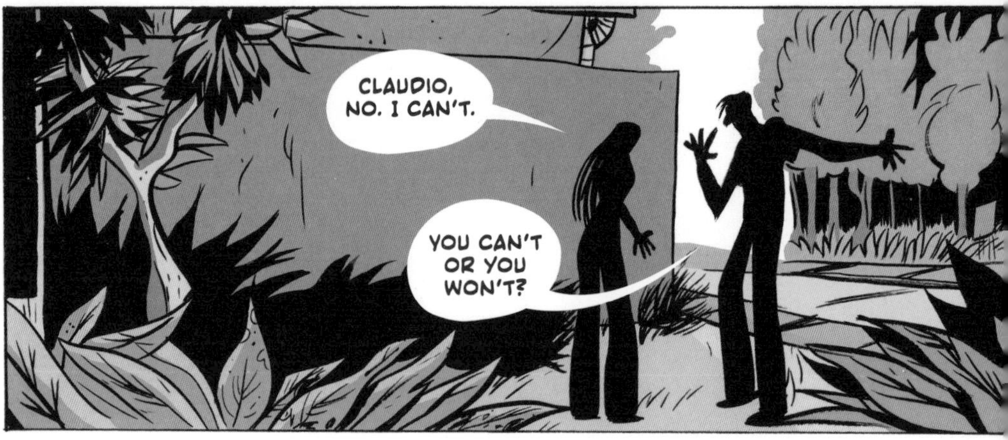
CLAUDIO,
NO. I CAN'T.
YOU CAN'T
OR YOU
WON'T?

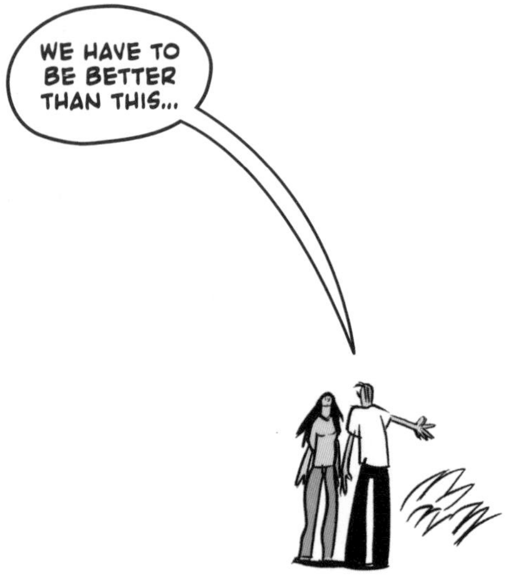
WE HAVE TO
BE BETTER
THAN THIS...

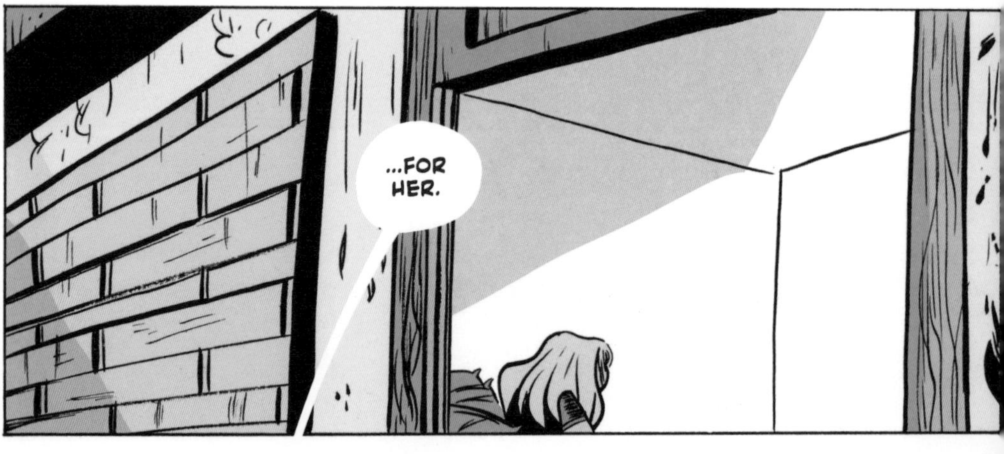
...FOR
HER.

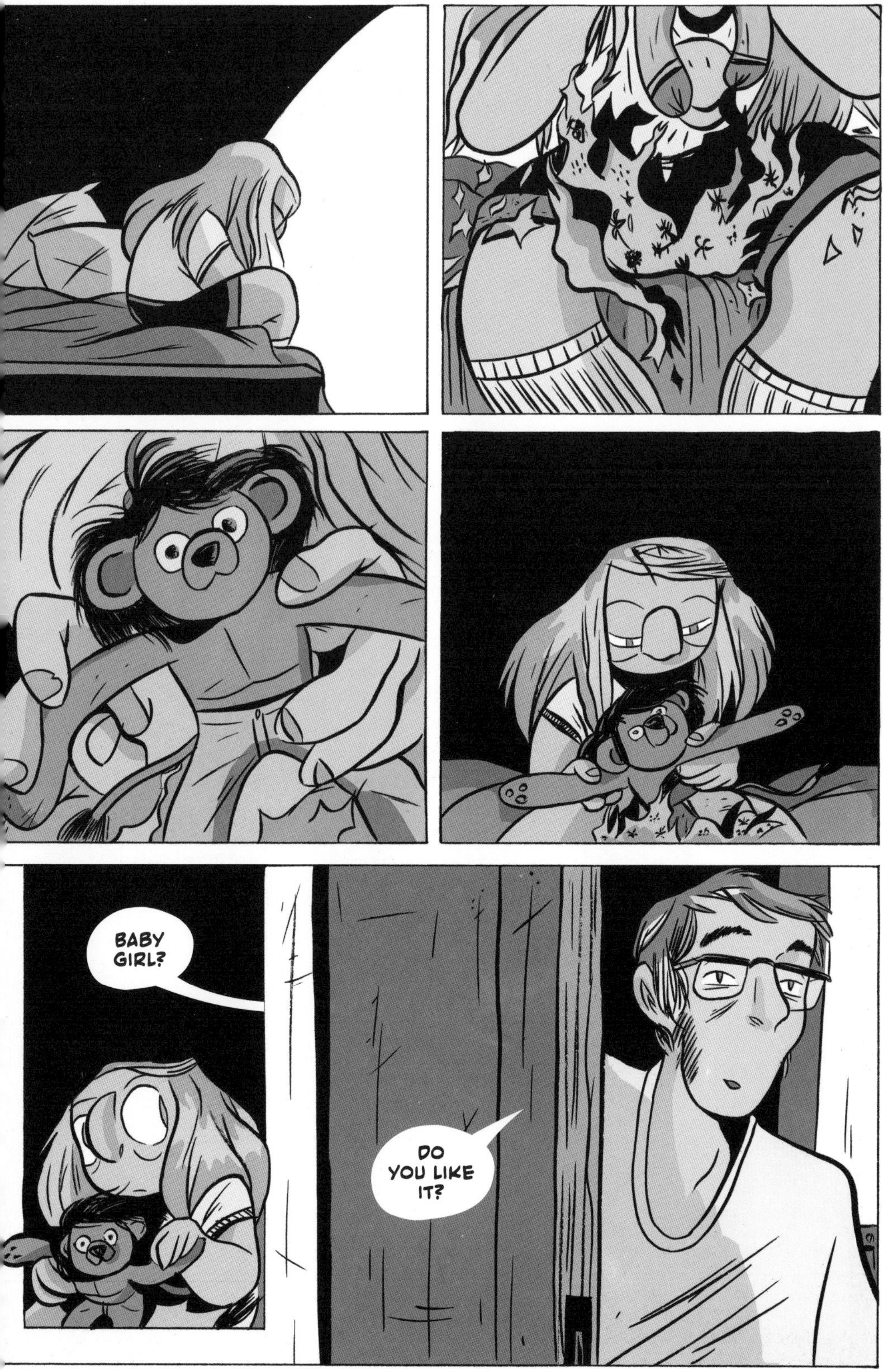
BABY GIRL?
DO YOU LIKE IT?

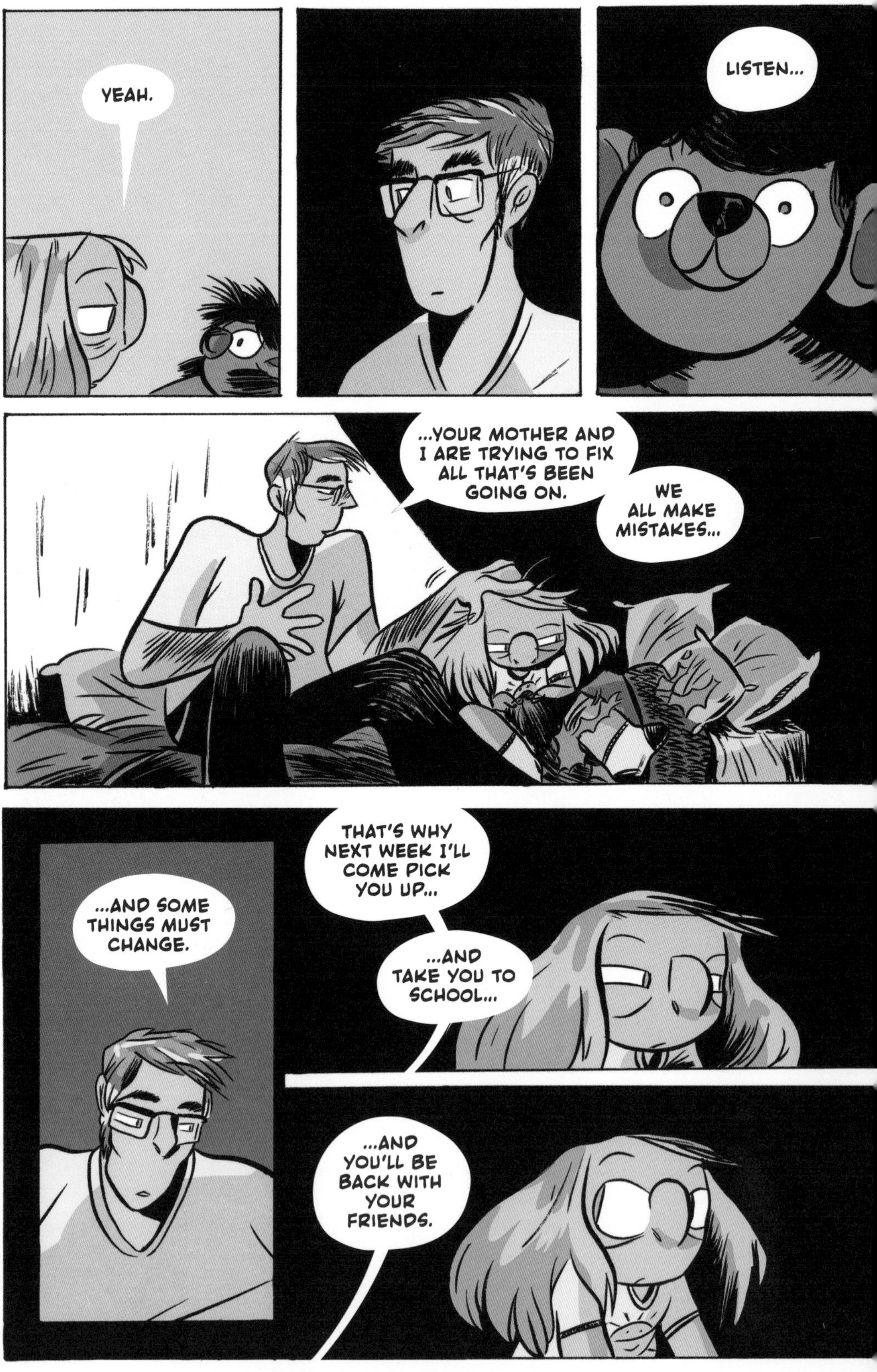
YEAH.
LISTEN...
...YOUR MOTHER AND I ARE TRYING TO FIX ALL THAT'S BEEN GOING ON.
WE ALL MAKE MISTAKES...
...AND SOME THINGS MUST CHANGE.
THAT'S WHY NEXT WEEK I'LL COME PICK YOU UP...
...AND TAKE YOU TO SCHOOL...
...AND YOU'LL BE BACK WITH YOUR FRIENDS.

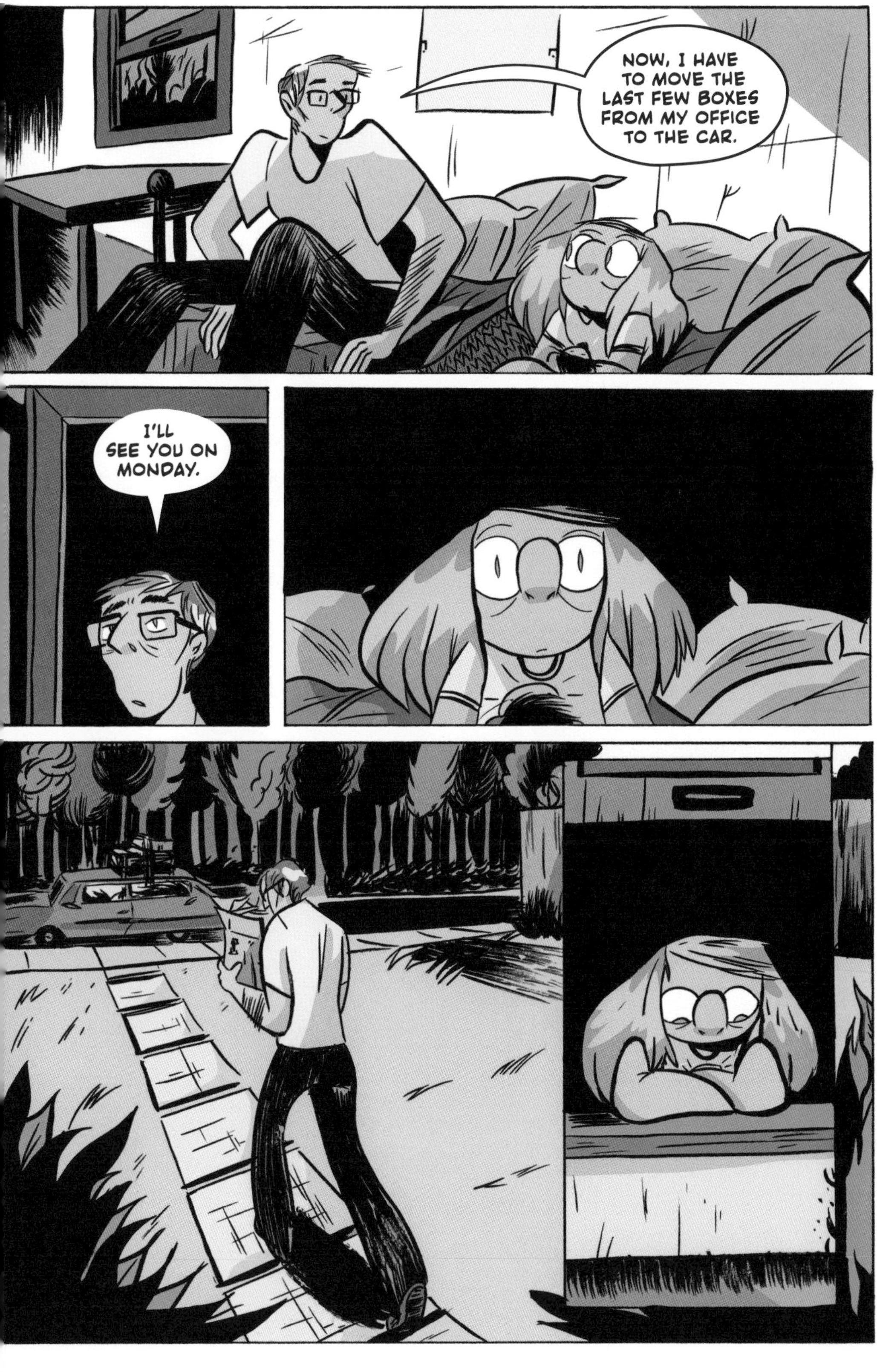
NOW, I HAVE TO MOVE THE LAST FEW BOXES FROM MY OFFICE TO THE CAR.
I'LL SEE YOU ON MONDAY.

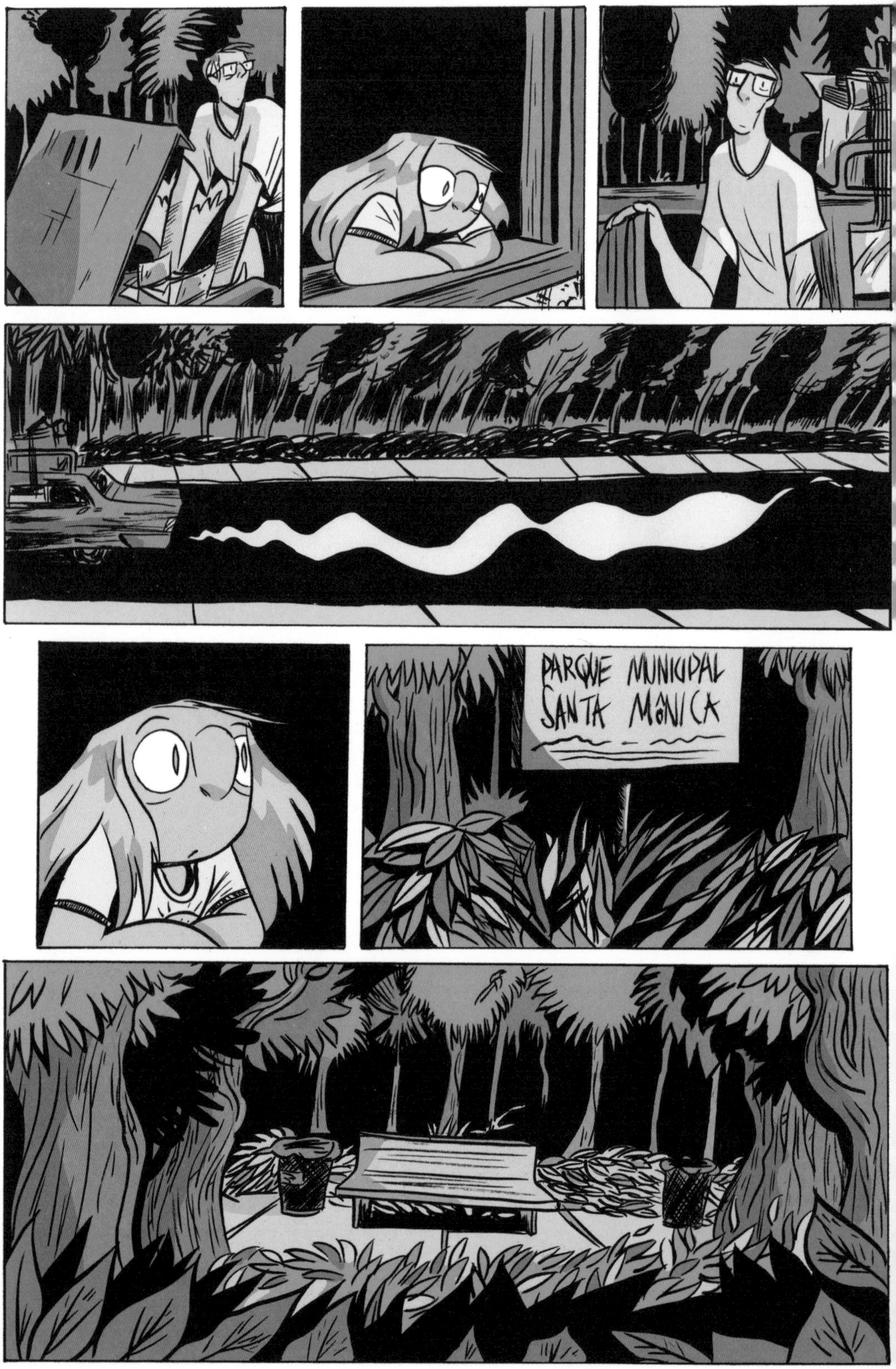
PARQUE MUNICIPAL
SANTA MÔNICA

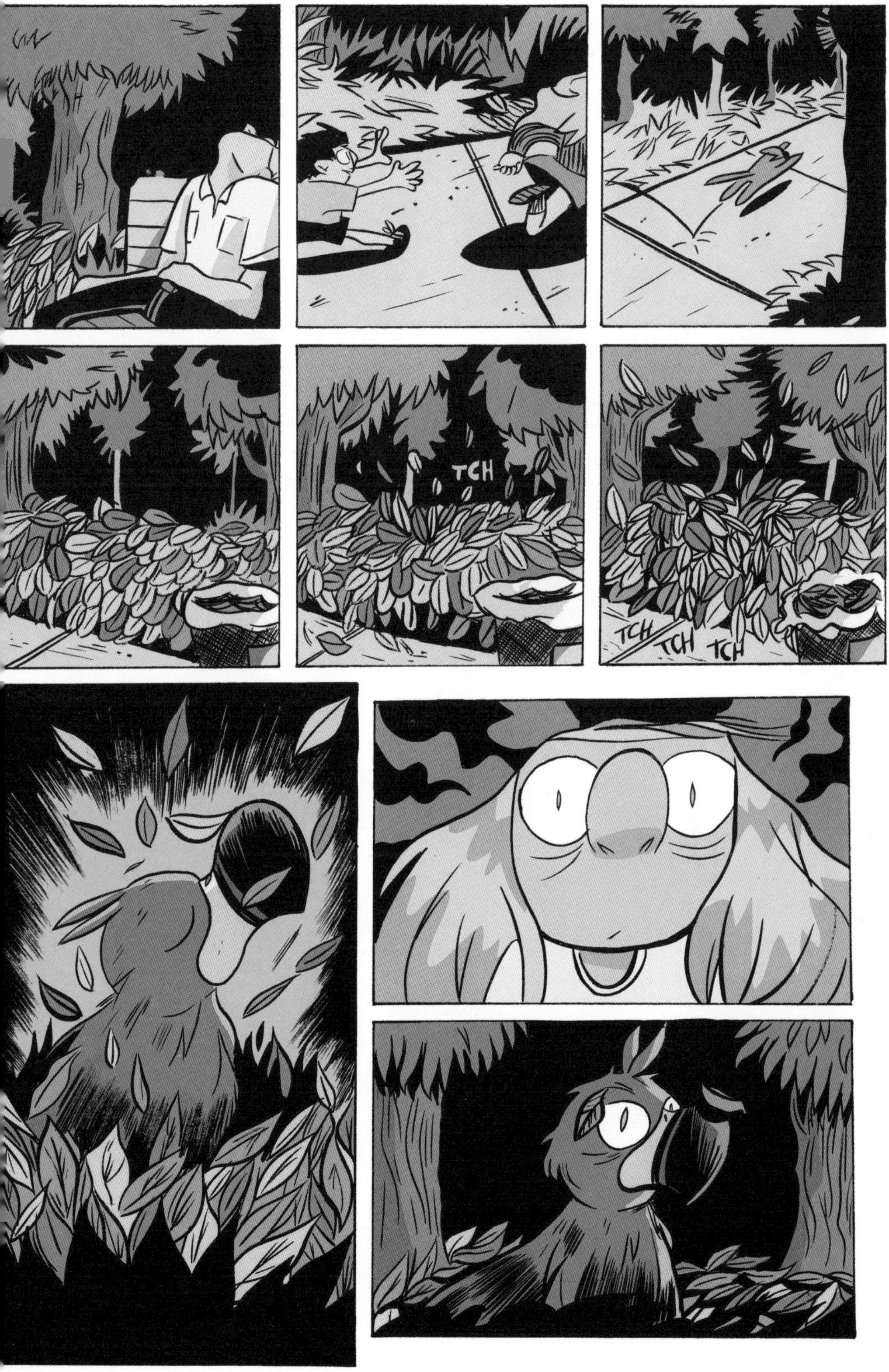
TCH
TCH
TCH
TCH

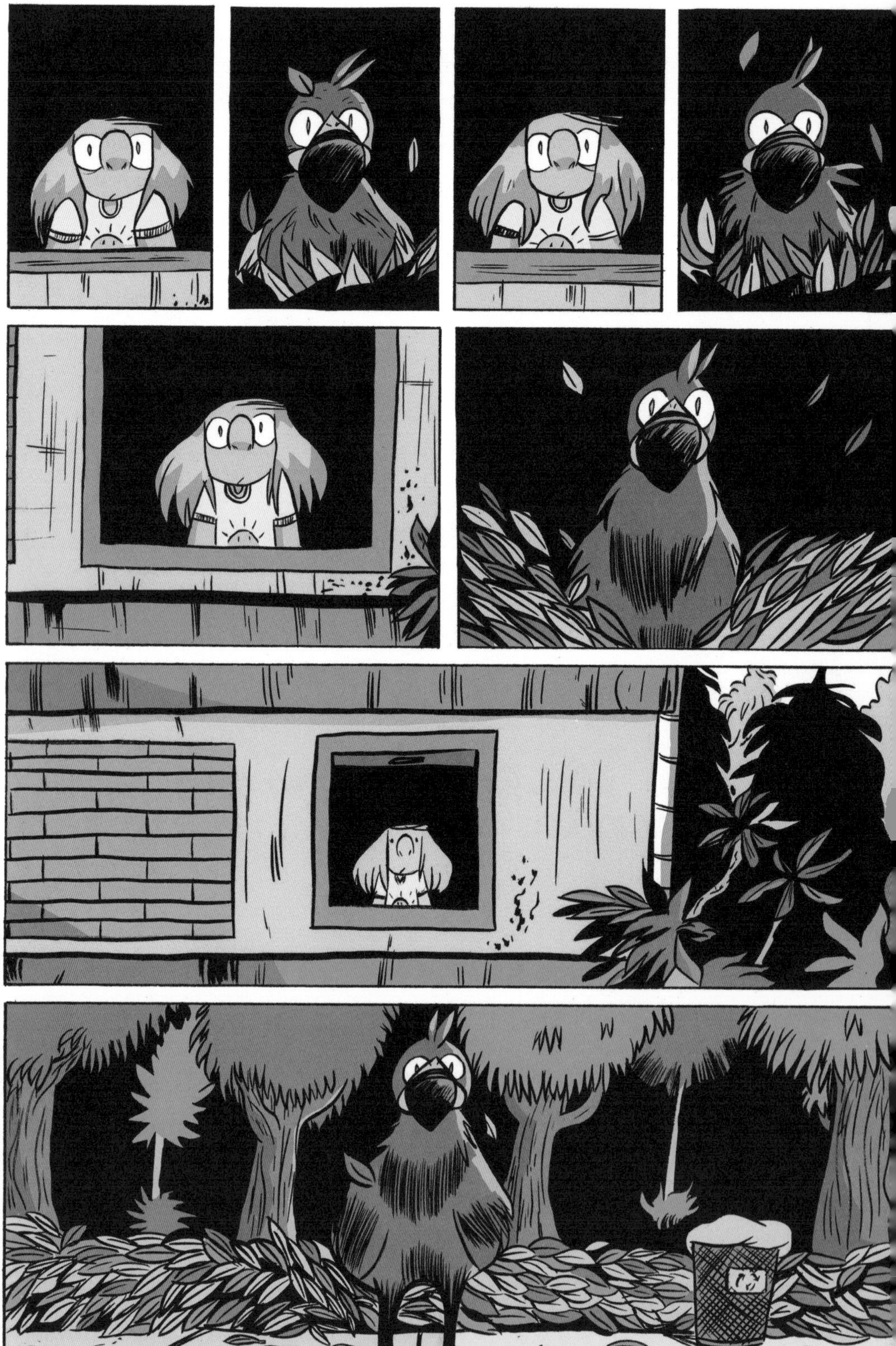

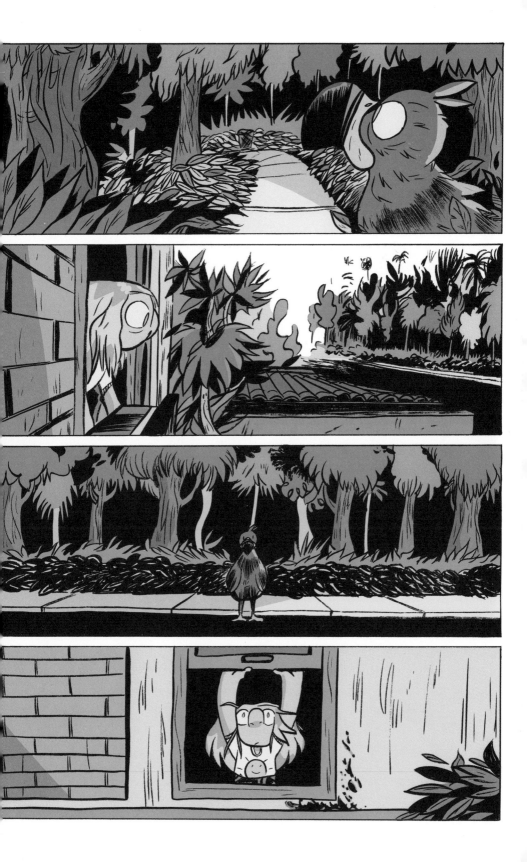

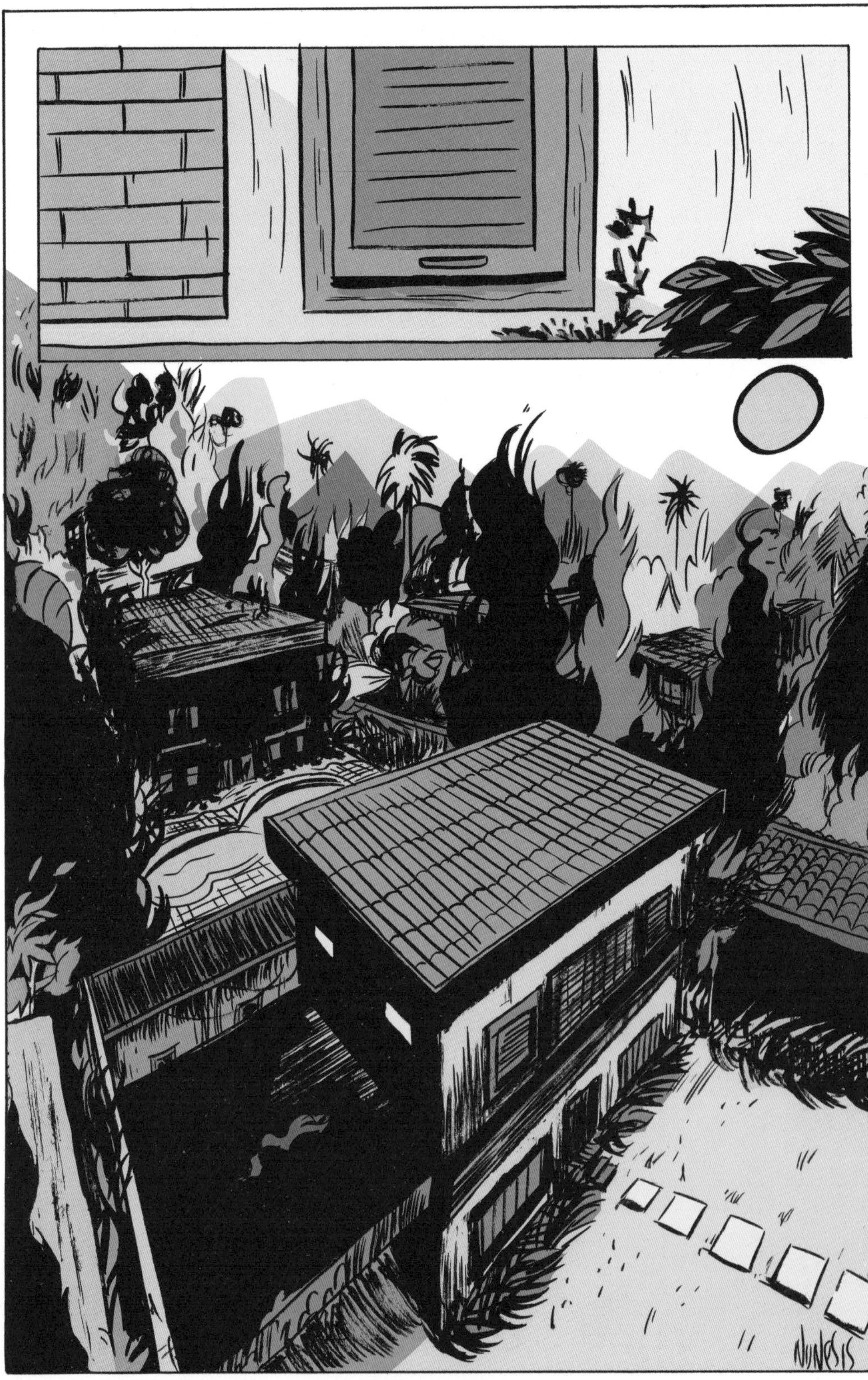
NUNESIS

FELIPE NUNES is a comic book artist and illustrator who began his career working at the studio of Fábio Moon and Gabriel Bá. Nunes' first published work, *SOS*, earned him an HQMIX nomination for Best Independent Author. *KLAUS*, his debut graphic novel, was published by Balão Editorial, and received an HQMIX award for New Drawing Talent. Nunes continues to work on independent comic books and graphic novels in his home country, Brazil.

DISCOVER
EXPLOSIVE NEW WORLDS

ADVENTURE TIME

Sam Sykes · Selina Espiritu · Sarah Stern
BRAVE CHEF BRIANNA

KELLY THOMPSON BRIANNE DROUHARD M. VICTORIA ROBADO
MEGA PRINCESS

THE NOT-SO SECRET SOCIETY
DALEY · CRAFTS · CLARK · BRUNI

OVER THE GARDEN WALL

STEVEN UNIVERSE
VOLUME ONE

Adventure Time
Pendleton Ward and Others
Volume 1
ISBN: 978-1-60886-280-1 | $14.99 US
Volume 2
ISBN: 978-1-60886-323-5 | $14.99 US
Adventure Time: Islands
ISBN: 978-1-60886-972-5 | $9.99 US

The Amazing World of Gumball
Ben Bocquelet and Others
Volume 1
ISBN: 978-1-60886-488-1 | $14.99 US
Volume 2
ISBN: 978-1-60886-793-6 | $14.99 US

Brave Chef Brianna
Sam Sykes, Selina Espiritu
ISBN: 978-1-68415-050-2 | $14.99 US

Mega Princess
Kelly Thompson, Brianne Drouhard
ISBN: 978-1-68415-007-6 | $14.99 US

The Not-So Secret Society
Matthew Daley, Arlene Daley, Wook Jin Clark
ISBN: 978-1-60886-997-8 | $9.99 US

Over the Garden Wall
Patrick McHale, Jim Campbell and Others
Volume 1
ISBN: 978-1-60886-940-4 | $14.99 US
Volume 2
ISBN: 978-1-68415-006-9 | $14.99 US

Steven Universe
Rebecca Sugar and Others
Volume 1
ISBN: 978-1-60886-706-6 | $14.99 US
Volume 2
ISBN: 978-1-60886-796-7 | $14.99 US

Steven Universe & The Crystal Gems
ISBN: 978-1-60886-921-3 | $14.99 US

Steven Universe: Too Cool for School
ISBN: 978-1-60886-771-4 | $14.99 US

kaboom!™

AVAILABLE AT YOUR LOCAL COMICS SHOP AND BOOKSTORE
To find a comics shop in your area, call 1-888-266-4226
WWW.**BOOM-STUDIOS**.COM